THE PELICAN SHAKESPEARE

GENERAL EDITOR ALFRED HARBAGE

THE LIFE OF
KING HENRY THE FIFTH

WILLIAM SHAKESPEARE

THE LIFE OF KING HENRY THE FIFTH

EDITED BY ALFRED HARBAGE

PENGUIN BOOKS

PENGUIN BOOKS
Published by the Penguin Group
Penguin Books USA Inc.,
375 Hudson Street, New York, New York 10014, U.S.A.
Penguin Books Ltd, 27 Wrights Lane,
London W8 5TZ, England
Penguin Books Australia Ltd, Ringwood,
Victoria, Australia
Penguin Books Canada Ltd, 10 Alcorn Avenue,
Toronto, Ontario, Canada M4V 3B2
Penguin Books (N.Z.) Ltd, 182–190 Wairau Road,
Auckland 10, New Zealand

Penguin Books Ltd, Registered Offices:
Harmondsworth, Middlesex, England

First published in *The Pelican Shakespeare* 1966
This revised edition first published 1972

15 17 19 20 18 16 14

Library of Congress catalog card number: 79-98365
ISBN 0 14 0714.09 X

Printed in the United States of America
Set in Monotype Ehrhardt

CONTENTS

PUBLISHER'S NOTE

Soon after the thirty-eight volumes forming *The Pelican Shakespeare* had been published, they were brought together in *The Complete Pelican Shakespeare*. The editorial revisions and new textual features are explained in detail in the General Editor's Preface to the one-volume edition. They have all been incorporated in the present volume. The following should be mentioned in particular:

The lines are not numbered in arbitrary units. Instead all lines are numbered which contain a word, phrase, or allusion explained in the glossarial notes. In the occasional instances where there is a long stretch of unannotated text, certain lines are numbered in italics to serve the conventional reference purpose.

The intrusive and often inaccurate place-headings inserted by early editors are omitted (as is becoming standard practise), but for the convenience of those who miss them, an indication of locale now appears as first item in the annotation of each scene.

In the interest of both elegance and utility, each speech-prefix is set in a separate line when the speaker's lines are in verse, except when these words form the second half of a pentameter line. Thus the verse form of the speech is kept visually intact, and turned-over lines are avoided. What is printed as verse and what is printed as prose has, in general, the authority of the original texts. Departures from the original texts in this regard have only the authority of editorial tradition and the judgment of the Pelican editors; and, in a few instances, are admittedly arbitrary.

SHAKESPEARE AND HIS STAGE

William Shakespeare was christened in Holy Trinity Church, Stratford-upon-Avon, April 26, 1564. His birth is traditionally assigned to April 23. He was the eldest of four boys and two girls who survived infancy in the family of John Shakespeare, glover and trader of Henley Street, and his wife Mary Arden, daughter of a small landowner of Wilmcote. In 1568 John was elected Bailiff (equivalent to Mayor) of Stratford, having already filled the minor municipal offices. The town maintained for the sons of the burgesses a free school, taught by a university graduate and offering preparation in Latin sufficient for university entrance; its early registers are lost, but there can be little doubt that Shakespeare received the formal part of his education in this school.

On November 27, 1582, a license was issued for the marriage of William Shakespeare (aged eighteen) and Ann Hathaway (aged twenty-six), and on May 26, 1583, their child Susanna was christened in Holy Trinity Church. The inference that the marriage was forced upon the youth is natural but not inevitable; betrothal was legally binding at the time, and was sometimes regarded as conferring conjugal rights. Two additional children of the marriage, the twins Hamnet and Judith, were christened on February 2, 1585. Meanwhile the prosperity of the elder Shakespeares had declined, and William was impelled to seek a career outside Stratford.

The tradition that he spent some time as a country

teacher is old but unverifiable. Because of the absence of records his early twenties are called the "lost years," and only one thing about them is certain – that at least some of these years were spent in winning a place in the acting profession. He may have begun as a provincial trouper, but by 1592 he was established in London and prominent enough to be attacked. In a pamphlet of that year, *Groats-worth of Wit*, the ailing Robert Greene complained of the neglect which university writers like himself had suffered from actors, one of whom was daring to set up as a playwright:

> . . . an vpstart Crow, beautified with our feathers, that with his *Tygers hart wrapt in a Players hyde*, supposes he is as well able to bombast out a blanke verse as the best of you: and beeing an absolute *Iohannes fac totum*, is in his owne conceit the onely Shake-scene in a countrey.

The pun on his name, and the parody of his line "O tiger's heart wrapped in a woman's hide" (*3 Henry VI*), pointed clearly to Shakespeare. Some of his admirers protested, and Henry Chettle, the editor of Greene's pamphlet, saw fit to apologize:

> . . . I am as sory as if the originall fault had beene my fault, because my selfe haue seene his demeanor no lesse ciuill than he excelent in the qualitie he professes: Besides, diuers of worship haue reported his vprightnes of dealing, which argues his honesty, and his facetious grace in writting, that approoues his Art. (Prefatory epistle, *Kind-Harts Dreame*)

The plague closed the London theatres for many months in 1592–94, denying the actors their livelihood. To this period belong Shakespeare's two narrative poems, *Venus and Adonis* and *The Rape of Lucrece*, both dedicated to the Earl of Southampton. No doubt the poet was rewarded with a gift of money as usual in such cases, but he did no further dedicating and we have no reliable information on whether Southampton, or anyone else, became his regular patron. His sonnets, first mentioned in 1598 and published without his consent in 1609, are intimate without being explicitly autobiographical. They seem to commemorate the poet's friendship with an idealized youth, rivalry with a more favored poet, and love affair with a dark mistress; and his bitterness when the mistress betrays him in conjunction with the friend; but it is difficult to decide precisely what the "story" is, impossible to decide whether it is fictional or true. The true distinction of the sonnets, at least of those not purely conventional, rests in the universality of the thoughts and moods they express, and in their poignancy and beauty.

In 1594 was formed the theatrical company known until 1603 as the Lord Chamberlain's men, thereafter as the King's men. Its original membership included, besides Shakespeare, the beloved clown Will Kempe and the famous actor Richard Burbage. The company acted in various London theatres and even toured the provinces, but it is chiefly associated in our minds with the Globe Theatre built on the south bank of the Thames in 1599. Shakespeare was an actor and joint owner of this company (and its Globe) through the remainder of his creative years. His plays, written at the average rate of two a year, together with Burbage's acting won it its place of leadership among the London companies.

Individual plays began to appear in print, in editions both honest and piratical, and the publishers became increasingly aware of the value of Shakespeare's name on the title pages. As early as 1598 he was hailed as the leading English dramatist in the *Palladis Tamia* of Francis Meres:

> As *Plautus* and *Seneca* are accounted the best for Comedy and Tragedy among the Latines, so *Shakespeare* among the English is the most excellent in both kinds for the stage: for Comedy, witnes his *Gentlemen of Verona*, his *Errors*, his *Loue labors lost*, his *Loue labours wonne* [at one time in print but no longer extant, at least under this title], his *Midsummers night dream*, & his *Merchant of Venice*; for Tragedy, his *Richard the 2*, *Richard the 3*, *Henry the 4*, *King Iohn*, *Titus Andronicus*, and his *Romeo and Iuliet*.

The note is valuable both in indicating Shakespeare's prestige and in helping us to establish a chronology. In the second half of his writing career, history plays gave place to the great tragedies; and farces and light comedies gave place to the problem plays and symbolic romances. In 1623, seven years after his death, his former fellow-actors, John Heminge and Henry Condell, cooperated with a group of London printers in bringing out his plays in collected form. The volume is generally known as the First Folio.

Shakespeare had never severed his relations with Stratford. His wife and children may sometimes have shared his London lodgings, but their home was Stratford. His son Hamnet was buried there in 1596, and his daughters Susanna and Judith were married there in 1607 and 1616 respectively. (His father, for whom he had secured a coat of arms and thus the privilege of writing himself gentleman, died in 1601, his mother in 1608.) His considerable earnings in London, as actor-sharer, part owner of the Globe, and playwright, were invested chiefly in Stratford property. In 1597 he purchased for £60 New Place, one of the two most imposing residences in the town. A number of other business transactions, as well as minor episodes in his career, have left documentary records. By 1611 he was in a position to retire, and he seems gradually to have withdrawn from theatrical activity in order to live in Stratford. In March, 1616, he made a will, leaving token bequests to Burbage, Heminge, and Condell, but the bulk of his estate to his family. The most famous feature of the will, the bequest of the second-best bed to his wife, reveals nothing about Shakespeare's marriage; the quaintness of the provision seems commonplace to those familiar with ancient testaments. Shakespeare died April 23, 1616, and was buried in the Stratford church where he had been christened. Within seven years a monument was erected to his memory on the north wall of the chancel. Its portrait bust and the Droeshout engraving on the title page of the First Folio provide the only likenesses with an established claim to authenticity. The best verbal vignette was written by his rival Ben Jonson, the more impressive for being imbedded in a context mainly critical:

> . . . I loved the man, and doe honour his memory (on this side idolatry) as much as any. Hee was indeed honest, and of an open and free nature: had an excellent Phantsie, brave notions, and gentle expressions. . . . (*Timber or Discoveries*, ca. 1623–30)

*

The reader of Shakespeare's plays is aided by a general knowledge of the way in which they were staged. The King's men acquired a roofed and artificially lighted theatre only toward the close of Shakespeare's career, and then only for winter use. Nearly all his plays were designed for performance in such structures as the Globe – a three-tiered amphitheatre with a large rectangular platform extending to the center of its yard. The plays were staged by daylight, by large casts brilliantly costumed, but with only a minimum of properties, without scenery, and quite possibly without intermissions. There was a rear stage gallery for action "above," and a curtained rear recess for "discoveries" and other special effects, but by far the major portion of any play was enacted upon the projecting platform, with episode following episode in swift succession, and with shifts of time and place signaled the audience only by the momentary clearing of the stage between the episodes. Information about the identity of the characters and, when necessary, about the time and place of the action was incorporated in the dialogue. No place-headings have been inserted in the present editions; these are apt to obscure the original fluidity of structure, with the emphasis upon action and speech rather than scenic background. (Indications of place are supplied in the footnotes.) The acting, including that of the youthful apprentices to the profession who performed the parts of women, was highly skillful, with a premium placed upon grace of gesture and beauty of diction. The audiences, a cross section of the general public, commonly numbered a thousand, sometimes more than two thousand. Judged by the type of plays they applauded, these audiences were not only large but also perceptive.

THE TEXTS OF THE PLAYS

About half of Shakespeare's plays appeared in print for the first time in the folio volume of 1623. The others had been published individually, usually in quarto volumes, during his lifetime or in the six years following his death. The copy used by the printers of the quartos varied greatly in merit, sometimes representing Shakespeare's true text, sometimes only a debased version of that text. The copy used by the printers of the folio also varied in merit, but was chosen with care. Since it consisted of the best available manuscripts, or the more acceptable quartos (although frequently in editions other than the first), or of quartos corrected by reference to manuscripts, we have good or reasonably good texts of most of the thirty-seven plays.

In the present series, the plays have been newly edited from quarto or folio texts, depending, when a choice offered, upon which is now regarded by bibliographical specialists as the more authoritative. The ideal has been to reproduce the chosen texts with as few alterations as possible, beyond occasional relineation, expansion of abbreviations, and modernization of punctuation and spelling. Emendation is held to a minimum, and such material as has been added, in the way of stage directions and lines supplied by an alternative text, has been enclosed in square brackets.

None of the plays printed in Shakespeare's lifetime were divided into acts and scenes, and the inference is that the author's own manuscripts were not so divided. In the folio collection, some of the plays remained undivided, some were divided into acts, and some were divided into acts and scenes. During the eighteenth century all of the plays were divided into acts and scenes, and in the Cambridge edition of the mid-nineteenth century, from which the influential Globe text derived, this division was more or less regularized and the lines were numbered. Many useful works of reference employ the act–scene–line apparatus thus established.

Since this act–scene division is obviously convenient, but is of very dubious authority so far as Shakespeare's own structural principles are concerned, or the original manner of staging his plays, a problem is presented to modern editors. In the present series the act–scene division is retained marginally, and may be viewed as a reference aid like the line numbering. A star marks the points of division when these points have been determined by a cleared stage indicating a shift of time and place in the action of the play, or when no harm results from the editorial assumption that there is such a shift. However, at those points where the established division is clearly misleading – that is, where continuous action has been split up into separate "scenes" – the star is omitted and the distortion corrected. This mechanical expedient seemed the best means of combining utility and accuracy.

THE GENERAL EDITOR

INTRODUCTION

The Epilogue to *2 Henry IV* promises that "our humble author will continue the story, with Sir John in it, and make you merry with fair Katherine of France" – will provide, in other words, more light entertainment spun out of Harry of Monmouth's famous victories and rollicking pastimes. This jovial preview little prepares us for the opening of *Henry V*:

> O for a Muse of fire, that would ascend
> The brightest heaven of invention;
> A kingdom for a stage, princes to act
> And monarchs to behold the swelling scene!

Still, the original promise is substantially kept. No other play of the Lancastrian trilogy so persistently bids for laughter, even though Sir John is *not* "in it." If this play were referred to Polonius, he might accurately classify it as "comical heroical."

There are various reasons why *Henry V* assumed its present curious form – in part dramatic epic, in part comic pastiche. The dramatic adventures of Prince and King Hal had in a measure been pre-selected, with Shakespeare bound by a theatrical tradition. *The Famous Victories of Henry V*, an anonymous play registered for publication in 1594 and printed in 1598, is a visible token of this tradition, presenting in crude outline most of the episodes, historical and fictitious, which reappear in *1 & 2 Henry IV* and, even more conspicuously, in *Henry V*. There had been stage treatments of Henry's career at least since 1588, and although the precise relation to them of the extant *Famous Victories* and Shakespeare's trilogy must remain conjectural, it is clear that audiences had come to expect fun as well as fireworks whenever Hal appeared. After 1598 these audiences preferred Sir John Falstaff as the funster in chief, and if he were denied them, the playwright must be liberal in providing substitutes. It has been argued that Falstaff was at first included in *Henry V* according to plan, in the role assigned in the present version to Pistol, but was deleted by death in order to placate the Brooke family, which still resented the fact that he had originally been named for its revered Lollard ancestor Sir John Oldcastle. This may be so, but to most readers the explosive ensign sounds Pistol-pure, and it is hard to imagine him as Sir John transmogrified.

A reason at least equally plausible for the exclusion of Falstaff is that he was a character to whom Henry could scarcely have remained aloof, and aloofness, at least to scalawag knights, would seem to be the order of the day for the pious and patriotic hero of Agincourt. Shakespeare had special reasons for sounding the high heroic note when *Henry V* was written. Not only would it be the capstone of his series of histories ascending through *Richard II* and *1 & 2 Henry IV* and descending through *1, 2, & 3 Henry VI* and *Richard III*, but the audiences of the moment were athirst for glory. Within the memory of most living men, the English had been ruled by a woman, and although loyal at heart to their Elizabeth, they had come to find something slightly dispiriting about an elderly woman and pacifist as the available royal image. Henry's image was that of a man and a warrior, endowed with eternal youth by virtue of his early death; and to intensify the emotions which his memory stirred there was the figure of the Earl of Essex leading, during the summer and fall of 1599, an English army in Ireland to put down Tyrone's rebellion. Henry's triumphant return from Agincourt evokes a reference to Essex in the fifth chorus of Shakespeare's play:

> Were now the general of our gracious empress,
> As in good time he may, from Ireland coming,
> Bringing rebellion broachèd on his sword,
> How many would the peaceful city quit
> To welcome him!

These lines provide us with the date of composition of *Henry V*, and a hint of the warlike spirit in London just before Essex proceeded to demonstrate how inglorious an English expedition could sometimes be.

Although Shakespeare may have worked hastily upon his play, and resorted to considerable patching (cf. II, Cho., 41–42 and note), he took its serious portions seriously, and went beyond the existing theatrical versions of Henry's career for his materials. He read with more than usual attentiveness the account of the reign in Holinshed, and turned for details to Hall and perhaps older chroniclers as well as to non-dramatic poets.

Before considering the portrait of Henry which Shakespeare produced, we had best come to what terms we can with the comic interludes. An inventory proves revealing: we have the preparation of Sir John's "staff" to follow and exploit the French wars, with a quarrel between Pistol and Nym (II, i); Hostess Quickly's report of Falstaff's death before his survivors shog off to the port of embarkation (II, iii); their reluctant participation in the assault on Harfleur, followed by a dispute in assorted dialects between Fluellen, Macmorris, and Jamy (III, ii); the English lesson of Princess Katherine (III, iv); Fluellen's quarrel with Pistol (first episode of III, vi); the Dauphin's infatuation with his horse, and the contest in proverb-capping between Orleans and the Constable of France (III, vii); Pistol's threat against Fluellen made to Henry incognito (middle episode of IV, i); further display of the Dauphin's fatuousness (IV, ii); Pistol's conquest of a cowardly

Frenchman (IV, iv); Fluellen's groping comparison of Henry and King Alexander (first episode in IV, vii); Fluellen's expression of devotion to the leek and to Henry and the latter's ruse in making him wear in his cap the glove offered by Williams as a gage (final episode in IV, vii); the averted conflict between Williams and Fluellen (first episode in IV, viii); Fluellen's forcing of Pistol to eat the leek worn in his cap, and Pistol's final deflation (V, i); Henry's bluff courtship of Katherine (middle episode, and bulk, of V, ii).

This implacably regular insertion of the comic episodes in alternate scenes would seem mechanical were it not for their diversity. Their diversity, on the other hand, and their fragmentary character, make the episodes seem gratuitous as compared with the comic matter in *1 & 2 Henry IV*. We may even mildly complain that either leeks or gloves, but not both, may be fittingly "worn" in the caps of a single play. Abundant enough already, the comedy of the play is often augmented in modern productions by making the Bishops of Ely and Canterbury senile (which they are not), the King of France a mental defective (which he may have been in fact, but is not in Shakespeare's portrayal), and the French lords ludicrously foppish as well as over-confident, although Shakespeare confers upon all except the Dauphin a fair degree of dignity. Although introduced adroitly enough, considering the unlikely setting in wartime courts and camps, the comic episodes cannot be considered neatly "thematic." The presence of the English, Welsh, Irish, and Scots captains in Henry's army has been taken as expressing an aspiration for British unity, but the portrait of Macmorris would scarcely propitiate the Irish, and that of Jamy is not favorable enough to offset the animadversions upon Scotland expressed by Henry and his counsellors early in the play. Gower and Fluellen, to be sure, are good and companionable men, but the union of the English and Welsh was more than an aspiration in 1599.

The contest for comic honors is between Pistol and Fluellen. We can understand why the former won the palm in contemporary esteem, as suggested by the title page of the first (and bad) quarto of 1600: *The Cronicle History of Henry the Fift. With his battel fought at Agin Court in France. Togither with Auntient Pistol.* While Bardolph's carbuncular face fails to project its pristine glow when there is only the Boy and not Falstaff to crack jests on it, and Nym's sullen "humors" lack variety, the dauntless fakery of Pistol and his on-beat rodomontade retains the true touch of Cheapside magic. Pistol's final passing drew a sigh from Dr Johnson. The Fluellen-funniness does not quite come off, at least in the reading, but it follows an interesting formula. Fluellen is an anti-Falstaff, not only in his unmasking of Pistol, who is serving as Falstaff's surrogate, but in his very character and personality. Fluellen is a ponderously dutiful non-wit, master of "the disciplines of the wars" but not of the English language, which issues from him like cold whey, whereas Falstaff had been a nimbly non-dutiful wit, master of nothing but brisk prose. Although Henry can safely associate with Fluellen, and we must give our moral approval to the substitution of good comic angel for bad comic angel, we cannot pretend that solemn respectability is as amusing as its reverse.

By common critical consent, the high moment in the comedy comes early and involves neither Pistol nor Fluellen, but the passing of Sir John Falstaff as reported by Hostess Nell. The wonder of the speech is that it hovers just this side of sacrilege (that side ribaldry) and yet is truly pathetic, with a touch of rough poetry. When this deplorable woman, who confuses Arthur and Abraham, and fails even to recognize the 23rd Psalm, speaks of having told the dying old sinner that he "should not think of God; I hoped there was no need to trouble himself with any such thoughts yet," we should recoil at the grim irony, but, strangely, we do not. She told him so "to comfort him." With every conceivable defect, moral as well as mental –

except bad nature – the Hostess is still godly after her fashion.

No doubt Shakespeare considered fun its own excuse for being, and his dissatisfaction with *Henry V*, expressed in prologue, epilogue, and choruses, had nothing to do with its motley. He felt, or professed to feel, that the resources of his theatre, indeed the dramatic form itself, were inadequate for the presentation of an epic theme. In epic fashion his "plot" concentrates on one great action – the victory at Agincourt – and all else in Henry's three actual invasions of France, spread over a period of five years, is ignored or made to serve merely as prelude and postlude to that victory. The choral speeches do not really, as they purport to do, fill in the historical record, but merely link together the chosen episodes so as to contribute to the epic sweep of the play. The size of the action is made the measure of the size of Henry, the epic hero, with everything contributing to his aggrandizement.

It is noteworthy, under the circumstances, that Henry has failed to win from readers anything like uniform approval, in fact has provoked occasional cold hostility. Certainly Shakespeare did not intentionally "undercut" his hero, any more than he intentionally "undercut" the glory of the English feat of arms by displaying the martial failings of Pistol, Bardolph, and Nym. Bardolph's exhortation (from a stationary position) "On, on, on, on, on! to the breach, to the breach!" follows like travesty immediately upon Henry's famous battle speech at Harfleur; and Pistol's mulcting of his captive is the only military exploit on the glorious field of Agincourt which we actually *see*. The intention is not parodic. If the effect is so, it is a consequence of the comical-heroical blend to which the playwright had committed himself. So far as the character of his hero is concerned, he had committed himself to something even more dangerous, a kind of religio-comical-heroical blend.

Henry V is a hard play to analyze in respect to intentional and unintentional effects. Ely and Canterbury provoke Henry to war in order to sidetrack a movement to expropriate church lands. In the course of their private discussion, they mention what may appeal to us (and may have appealed to sixteenth-century Englishmen) as some very good economic and charitable results of such expropriation, and yet if we approve of Henry's conquest, we must presumably approve of their ruse. Why did Shakespeare choose to include this matter from his sources when there was so much else which he excluded? Was Henry to be shown as now so pious that he took suggestion from holy men without reflecting that they might act from somewhat less than holy motives? He sternly adjures them to speak the truth, so far as the legality of his claim to France is concerned, but he displays no curiosity about their present interest in it. Perhaps we are intended to conclude that if high churchmen approve of war, it would be too much to expect their royal parishioner to do otherwise.

The "faults" which critics have found in Henry are really the side-effects of Shakespeare's having tried to do too much for him – by conferring upon him incompatible virtues. He is the religious convert, the pattern of a Christian Prince – morally impeccable, careful of his subjects by whom he is beloved, and highly competent in his judicial and administrative capacity. But at the same time that he exemplifies Christian virtue, he also exemplifies non-Christian *virtu* – that of pagan conquerors like Alexander and Caesar, or medieval champions like Hotspur, by whose light "Did all the chivalry of England move / To do brave acts." As blatantly as Hotspur he confesses that he is as covetous of "honor" as the "most offending soul alive." He proclaims that

> In peace there's nothing so becomes a man
> As modest stillness and humility,
> But when the blast of war blows in our ears,
> Then imitate the action of the tiger.

Presumably the opposite types of virtue are adaptable to the opposite conditions of peace and war, but the fact stands that Henry chooses war. A man of peace cannot be a man of war unless his own nation is under attack. Henry is not the attacked but the attacker. It is the King of France who shows a disposition to negotiate, with the offer of his daughter's hand and, in Henry's view, some "petty and unprofitable dukedoms." Now it is quite true that the historical Henry and his nation considered his cause just, but it is difficult for us to grow excited about the illegality of the Salic law, or the eagerness of a litigant to recover family property. It is impossible for us to consider his cause religious. But Henry, the religious man and humane ruler, is obliged to think of his war as a crusade, and his assumption taints the air.

At the same time that he loves this war, he loathes war in general. The expression of loathing takes the form of listing its horrors and holding others responsible for them – the Archbishop of Canterbury if he wrongly "incites" him, the Dauphin for sending him a "mock," the citizens of Harfleur if they resist, and so on. It is impossible for the religious wielder of a secular sword to do anything quite to our satisfaction. Even Henry's modesty comes under question. He attributes the victory at Agincourt to God, but we might prefer a claim of personal prowess to a claim of special influence with God. Henry's incompatible virtues sometimes produce the effect of duplicity since his actions and words contend with each other, as when he preaches at the Dauphin and the French in general about provocations which are not the true cause of the war, or when he orders the slaying of the French prisoners (as a justifiable military measure) and then, retroactively (unless this is a defect in the text of the play), speaks of it as retaliation for the French attack on the camp-boys – "I was not angry since I came to France / Until this instant." The killing of the prisoners, though an historical fact, has caused Henry's admirers more concern than anything else. The true fault is that Henry is not permitted by the over-zealous playwright to wear his religio-moral and military haloes turn and turn about, but is forced to wear them both at once.

Finally, Henry is given a quality, intermittently displayed, which is compatible neither with the "modest stillness and humility" proper to peace, nor the "action of the tiger" proper to war. He must be shown as an informal, humorous "regular guy" – a self-styled "king of good fellows." He interrupts his reflections upon God's grace in visiting carnage upon the French in order to play a friendly practical joke on Fluellen, and he courts Princess Katherine with a manly bluntness which is ultimately a trial to our nerves. It contains amusing matter, but it does go on and on; never has anyone advertised his inarticulateness with such loquacity.

Henry is, in fact, the victim of Shakespeare's good will. It is somewhat naive to mistake defects in the playwright's conception for defects in Henry's personal character. More in the true spirit of the play is another kind of naiveté – the fervor of the patriotic Englishman as he contemplates Agincourt and Shakespeare's tribute to its hero. The nineteenth-century American was little inclined to grow analytical about the portrait of George Washington produced by Parson Weems, and Weems was something less than a literary genius. In its fine moments *Henry V* expresses perfectly the spirit (including perhaps the sense of divine call) of a little nation with a great history:

> O England! model to thy inward greatness,
> Like little body with a mighty heart....

The play is also able to achieve a foreign conquest of its own, and to stir non-English hearts. If Henry is the aggressor, he is also the underdog, and his devotion to his purpose confers a kind of purity upon him and his tattered host. The choruses, which show that Shakespeare might have succeeded where other Elizabethans failed – in writing an epic poem – dazzle with their descriptions of the youth of England selling "the pasture now to buy the horse," the brave fleet "on th' inconstant billows dancing," the remnant army with "lank-lean cheeks and war-worn coats" as "by their watchful fires" they "Sit patiently and inly ruminate."

The chorus and early scenes of Act IV are admirable. As Henry in disguise shares the watch of Bates, Court, and Williams, and utters his troubled defense of kingship, we are expected to reflect upon what a fine monarch he is. We must try to do so. But it requires no effort for us to reflect upon what fine subjects he has. There is something amazingly modern about Bates, Court, and Williams. Unique in their day as straight portraits of common soldiers, they have become the prototypes of such in a host of British war dramas and motion pictures. Grumpy, undemonstrative, unillusioned, they are still men of tenacious faith – resolved to trust their leaders and to do their duty well. Their character more than Henry's explains the victory at Agincourt. Henry himself grows in appeal as he accepts the loneliness of leadership and kneels in solitary prayer. For once he escapes self-righteousness.

Henry's address at Agincourt is in a class by itself as inspirational poetry. It is a different kind of thing from the battle oration before Harfleur, because it defines the moral value, perhaps the only moral value, which battle can develop. The *comitatus* is restored, and for a moment the high and the low, the leaders and the led, come together as a unit in mutual interdependence, trust, and admiration. The great day is seen prophetically as a point in history –

> Old men forget; yet all shall be forgot,
> But he'll remember, with advantages,
> What feats he did that day.

No one, English or non-English, can read the lines and fail to "rouse him at the name of Crispian" or escape a momentary pang of regret that he could not have been one of that "happy few" who on that day were able (Pistol excepted) to "gentle" their condition. The late John Kennedy was neither English nor recognizably kin to Macmorris, but when Shakespeare entered the White House in the brave new days of 1961, Henry's speech at Agincourt was the Shakespearean passage which this young leader was most eager once more to hear.

Harvard University ALFRED HARBAGE

NOTE ON THE TEXT

King Henry the Fifth was first printed in a quarto of 1600 in "cut" and corrupted form, and this version was twice reprinted. A much-improved version was printed in the folio of 1623, evidently from pages of the later quartos corrected by reference to the author's draft. The present edition is based on the folio text on principles explained in the Appendix. The quarto text is not divided into acts and scenes. The folio text is divided, imperfectly, into acts; the relation of this division to the one supplied marginally in the present edition is indicated in the Appendix.

THE LIFE OF KING HENRY THE FIFTH

[NAMES OF THE ACTORS

Chorus
King Henry the Fifth
Dukes of Gloucester and Bedford, brothers of the King
Duke of Exeter, uncle of the King
Duke of York, cousin of the King
Earls of Salisbury, Westmoreland, Warwick, and Cambridge
Archbishop of Canterbury
Bishop of Ely
Lord Scroop
Sir Thomas Grey
Sir Thomas Erpingham
Gower, Fluellen, Macmorris, Jamy, officers in the English army
John Bates, Alexander Court, Michael Williams, soldiers in the English army
Pistol, Nym, Bardolph
Boy
An English Herald
Charles the Sixth, King of France
Lewis, the Dauphin
Dukes of Burgundy, Orleans, Bourbon, and Britaine
The Constable of France
Rambures, Grandpré, French lords
Governor of Harfleur
Montjoy, a French herald
Ambassadors to King Henry
Isabel, Queen of France
Katherine, daughter of the French King and Queen
Alice, an attendant to Katherine
Hostess Quickly of an Eastcheap tavern, wedded to Pistol
Lords, Ladies, Officers, Soldiers, Citizens, Messengers, and Attendants

Scene: *England and France*]

THE LIFE OF KING HENRY THE FIFTH

Enter Prologue. Pro.

O for a Muse of fire, that would ascend
The brightest heaven of invention;
A kingdom for a stage, princes to act
And monarchs to behold the swelling scene!
Then should the warlike Harry, like himself,
Assume the port of Mars, and at his heels,
Leashed in like hounds, should famine, sword, and fire
Crouch for employment. But pardon, gentles all,
The flat unraisèd spirits that hath dared
On this unworthy scaffold to bring forth
So great an object. Can this cockpit hold
The vasty fields of France? Or may we cram
Within this wooden O the very casques
That did affright the air at Agincourt?
O, pardon! since a crooked figure may
Attest in little place a million;
And let us, ciphers to this great accompt,
On your imaginary forces work.

Pro. 1 *fire* (most buoyant of the four elements: earth, water, air, fire; the one which ascended to the empyrean) 2 *invention* creative imagination 4 *swelling* increasing in grandeur 5 *like* in a manner worthy of 6 *port* bearing 9 *unraisèd* unleavened 10 *scaffold* stage 13 *wooden O* circular theatre (depreciatory, like *cockpit* at l. 11); *the very casques* i.e. even the helmets 15 *crooked figure* cipher (which can raise 100,000 to 1,000,000) 17 *accompt* (1) story, (2) reckoning (continuing the word-play on 'cipher' initiated by *wooden O*)

Suppose within the girdle of these walls
Are now confined two mighty monarchies,
21 Whose high-upreared and abutting fronts
22 The perilous narrow ocean parts asunder.
Piece out our imperfections with your thoughts:
Into a thousand parts divide one man
25 And make imaginary puissance.
Think, when we talk of horses, that you see them
Printing their proud hoofs i' th' receiving earth;
28 For 'tis your thoughts that now must deck our kings,
Carry them here and there, jumping o'er times,
Turning th' accomplishment of many years
31 Into an hourglass – for the which supply,
Admit me Chorus to this history,
Who, Prologue-like, your humble patience pray,
Gently to hear, kindly to judge, our play. *Exit.*

I, i *Enter the two Bishops, [the Archbishop] of Canterbury and [the Bishop of] Ely.*

CANTERBURY
1 My lord, I'll tell you, that self bill is urged
Which in th' eleventh year of the last king's reign
Was like, and had indeed against us passed
4 But that the scambling and unquiet time
5 Did push it out of farther question.

ELY
But how, my lord, shall we resist it now?

CANTERBURY
It must be thought on. If it pass against us,
We lose the better half of our possession;

21 *abutting fronts* frontiers 22 *perilous . . . ocean* i.e. English Channel 25 *puissance* armed forces 28 *deck* array 31 *hourglass* i.e. short measure of time; *for . . . supply* in aid whereof

I, i Within the palace of the King of England 1 *self* selfsame 4 *scambling* snatching, predatory 5 *question* discussion

For all the temporal lands which men devout
By testament have given to the Church
Would they strip from us; being valued thus –
As much as would maintain, to the king's honor,
Full fifteen earls and fifteen hundred knights,
Six thousand and two hundred good esquires,
And to relief of lazars, and weak age
Of indigent faint souls past corporal toil,
A hundred almshouses right well supplied;
And to the coffers of the king beside
A thousand pounds by th' year. Thus runs the bill.

ELY
This would drink deep.

CANTERBURY 'Twould drink the cup and all.

ELY
But what prevention?

CANTERBURY
The king is full of grace and fair regard.

ELY
And a true lover of the holy Church.

CANTERBURY
The courses of his youth promised it not.
The breath no sooner left his father's body
But that his wildness, mortified in him,
Seemed to die too. Yea, at that very moment
Consideration like an angel came
And whipped th' offending Adam out of him,
Leaving his body as a paradise
T' envelop and contain celestial spirits.
Never was such a sudden scholar made;
Never came reformation in a flood
With such a heady currance scouring faults;
Nor never Hydra-headed willfulness

9 *temporal* in secular use 15 *lazars* lepers 26 *mortified* struck dead 28 *Consideration* penitent reflection 32 *scholar* i.e. man of disciplined mind 34 *heady currance* headlong current 35 *Hydra* the monster with proliferating heads slain by Hercules at Lerna

36 So soon did lose his seat – and all at once –
As in this king.

ELY We are blessèd in the change.

CANTERBURY

Hear him but reason in divinity
And, all-admiring, with an inward wish
You would desire the king were made a prelate;
Hear him debate of commonwealth affairs,
You would say it hath been all in all his study;
List his discourse of war, and you shall hear
A fearful battle rend'red you in music;
45 Turn him to any cause of policy,
46 The Gordian knot of it he will unloose,
47 Familiar as his garter; that when he speaks,
48 The air, a chartered libertine, is still,
49 And the mute wonder lurketh in men's ears
To steal his sweet and honeyed sentences;
51 So that the art and practic part of life
Must be the mistress to this theoric;
Which is a wonder how his grace should glean it,
Since his addiction was to courses vain,
His companies unlettered, rude, and shallow,
His hours filled up with riots, banquets, sports;
And never noted in him any study,
Any retirement, any sequestration
59 From open haunts and popularity.

ELY

The strawberry grows underneath the nettle,
And wholesome berries thrive and ripen best
Neighbored by fruit of baser quality;
And so the prince obscured his contemplation

36 *his seat* its throne 45 *cause of policy* political issue 46 *Gordian knot* intricate knot cut by Alexander in asserting his destiny to rule over Asia 47 *Familiar* offhandedly, mechanically 48 *chartered* licensed; *libertine* one free from bondage or restraint 49 *mute wonder* silent wonderer 51–52 *the art . . . theoric* i.e. study and practise must be the teacher of this mastery of theory 59 *open haunts* places of public resort; *popularity* low company

Under the veil of wildness, which, no doubt,
Grew like the summer grass, fastest by night,
Unseen, yet crescive in his faculty.

CANTERBURY
It must be so, for miracles are ceased
And therefore we must needs admit the means
How things are perfected.

ELY
But, my good lord,
How now for mitigation of this bill
Urged by the commons? Doth his majesty
Incline to it or no?

CANTERBURY
He seems indifferent,
Or rather swaying more upon our part
Than cherishing th' exhibiters against us;
For I have made an offer to his majesty,
Upon our spiritual Convocation
And in regard of causes now in hand
Which I have opened to his grace at large
As touching France, to give a greater sum
Than ever at one time the clergy yet
Did to his predecessors part withal.

ELY
How did this offer seem received, my lord?

CANTERBURY
With good acceptance of his majesty,
Save that there was not time enough to hear,
As I perceived his grace would fain have done,
The severals and unhidden passages
Of his true titles to some certain dukedoms,
And generally to the crown and seat of France
Derived from Edward his great-grandfather.

ELY
What was th' impediment that broke this off?

66 *crescive . . . faculty* i.e. given to growth 68 *means* i.e. natural means 74 *exhibiters* introducers of the bill 76 *Upon* on behalf of 86 *severals* particulars; *unhidden passages* open transmission 89 *Edward* i.e. King Edward III

CANTERBURY

The French ambassador upon that instant
Craved audience; and the hour I think is come
To give him hearing. Is it four o'clock?

ELY

It is.

CANTERBURY

Then go we in to know his embassy,
Which I could with a ready guess declare
Before the Frenchman speak a word of it.

ELY

I'll wait upon you, and I long to hear it. *Exeunt.*

*

I, ii *Enter the King, Humphrey [Duke of Gloucester], Bedford, Clarence, Warwick, Westmoreland, and Exeter [with Attendants].*

KING

Where is my gracious Lord of Canterbury?

EXETER

Not here in presence.

KING Send for him, good uncle.

WESTMORELAND

Shall we call in th' ambassador, my liege?

KING

4 Not yet, my cousin. We would be resolved,
Before we hear him, of some things of weight
6 That task our thoughts concerning us and France.

Enter two Bishops [the Archbishop of Canterbury and the Bishop of Ely].

CANTERBURY

God and his angels guard your sacred throne
And make you long become it!

I, ii The presence chamber of the palace **s.d.** *Clarence* (a 'ghost' character, mute and appearing only in this single stage direction) **4** *resolved* freed from doubt **6** *task* burden

KING Sure we thank you.
My learnèd lord, we pray you to proceed
And justly and religiously unfold
Why the Law Salic, that they have in France,
Or should or should not bar us in our claim. 12
And God forbid, my dear and faithful lord,
That you should fashion, wrest, or bow your reading,
Or nicely charge your understanding soul 15
With opening titles miscreate, whose right 16
Suits not in native colors with the truth;
For God doth know how many now in health
Shall drop their blood in approbation 19
Of what your reverence shall incite us to.
Therefore take heed how you impawn our person, 21
How you awake our sleeping sword of war
We charge you in the name of God take heed;
For never two such kingdoms did contend
Without much fall of blood, whose guiltless drops
Are every one a woe, a sore complaint 26
'Gainst him whose wrongs gives edge unto the swords 27
That makes such waste in brief mortality.
Under this conjuration speak, my lord;
For we will hear, note, and believe in heart
That what you speak is in your conscience washed
As pure as sin with baptism. 32

CANTERBURY
Then hear me, gracious sovereign, and you peers,
That owe yourselves, your lives, and services
To this imperial throne. There is no bar
To make against your highness' claim to France
But this which they produce from Pharamond: 37
'In terram Salicam mulieres ne succedant';

12 *Or* either **15** *nicely . . . soul* subtly impugn your rational faculty; i.e. rationalize **16–17** *opening . . . colors* advancing illegitimate claims, the validity of which fails to harmonize **19** *approbation* support **21** *impawn* engage **26** *woe* grievance **27** *wrongs* wrongdoing **32** *sin* original sin **37** *Pharamond* legendary Frankish king

'No woman shall succeed in Salic land.'
Which Salic land the French unjustly gloze
To be the realm of France, and Pharamond
The founder of this law and female bar.
Yet their own authors faithfully affirm
That the land Salic is in Germany,
Between the floods of Sala and of Elbe;
46 Where Charles the Great, having subdued the Saxons,
There left behind and settled certain French;
Who, holding in disdain the German women
49 For some dishonest manners of their life,
Established then this law: to wit, no female
Should be inheritrix in Salic land;
Which Salic, as I said, 'twixt Elbe and Sala
Is at this day in Germany called Meisen.
Then doth it well appear the Salic Law
Was not devisèd for the realm of France;
Nor did the French possess the Salic land
Until four hundred one and twenty years
58 After defunction of King Pharamond,
Idly supposed the founder of this law,
Who died within the year of our redemption
Four hundred twenty-six; and Charles the Great
Subdued the Saxons, and did seat the French
Beyond the river Sala, in the year
Eight hundred five. Besides, their writers say,
King Pepin, which deposèd Childeric,
Did, as heir general, being descended
Of Blithild, which was daughter to King Clothair,
Make claim and title to the crown of France.
Hugh Capet also, who usurped the crown
Of Charles the Duke of Lorraine, sole heir male
Of the true line and stock of Charles the Great,
72 To find his title with some shows of truth,
Though in pure truth it was corrupt and naught,

46 *Charles the Great* Charlemagne 49 *dishonest* unchaste 58 *defunction* death 72 *find* furnish

Conveyed himself as th' heir to th' Lady Lingard,
Daughter to Charlemain, who was the son 75
To Lewis the Emperor, and Lewis the son
Of Charles the Great. Also King Lewis the Tenth, 77
Who was sole heir to the usurper Capet,
Could not keep quiet in his conscience,
Wearing the crown of France, till satisfied
That fair Queen Isabel, his grandmother,
Was lineal of the Lady Ermengard,
Daughter to Charles the foresaid Duke of Lorraine;
By the which marriage the line of Charles the Great
Was reunited to the crown of France.
So that, as clear as is the summer's sun,
King Pepin's title and Hugh Capet's claim,
King Lewis his satisfaction, all appear 88
To hold in right and title of the female:
So do the kings of France unto this day.
Howbeit they would hold up this Salic Law
To bar your highness claiming from the female,
And rather choose to hide them in a net 93
Than amply to imbar their crooked titles 94
Usurped from you and your progenitors.

KING
May I with right and conscience make this claim?

CANTERBURY
The sin upon my head, dread sovereign!
For in the Book of Numbers is it writ: 98
When the man dies, let the inheritance
Descend unto the daughter. Gracious lord,
Stand for your own, unwind your bloody flag,
Look back into your mighty ancestors;
Go, my dread lord, to your great-grandsire's tomb,
From whom you claim; invoke his warlike spirit,

75, 77 *Charlemain, Lewis the Tenth* (actually Charles the Bald and Louis IX; errors repeated from the chronicles) 88 *his satisfaction* i.e. King Lewis's conviction 93 *net* i.e. web of sophistry 94 *imbar* bar claim to, impeach 98 *Numbers* (see Numbers xxvii, 8)

And your great-uncle's, Edward the Black Prince,
106 Who on the French ground played a tragedy,
Making defeat on the full power of France,
Whiles his most mighty father on a hill
Stood smiling to behold his lion's whelp
110 Forage in blood of French nobility.
111 O noble English, that could entertain
With half their forces the full pride of France
And let another half stand laughing by,
114 All out of work and cold for action!

ELY
Awake remembrance of these valiant dead,
116 And with your puissant arm renew their feats.
You are their heir; you sit upon their throne;
118 The blood and courage that renownèd them
Runs in your veins; and my thrice-puissant liege
Is in the very May-morn of his youth,
Ripe for exploits and mighty enterprises.

EXETER
Your brother kings and monarchs of the earth
Do all expect that you should rouse yourself
As did the former lions of your blood.

WESTMORELAND
They know your grace hath cause, and means, and might –
126 So hath your highness! Never king of England
Had nobles richer and more loyal subjects,
Whose hearts have left their bodies here in England
129 And lie pavilioned in the fields of France.

CANTERBURY
O, let their bodies follow, my dear liege,
With blood, and sword, and fire to win your right!
132 In aid whereof we of the spiritualty

106 *tragedy* i.e. Battle of Crécy, 1346 **110** *Forage in* prey on **111** *entertain* engage **114** *action* i.e. inaction **116** *puissant* powerful **118** *renownèd* brought renown to **126** *So* so indeed **129** *pavilioned* in tents of war **132** *spiritualty* clergy

Will raise your highness such a mighty sum
As never did the clergy at one time
Bring in to any of your ancestors.

KING

We must not only arm t' invade the French,
But lay down our proportions to defend 137
Against the Scot, who will make road upon us 138
With all advantages. 139

CANTERBURY

They of those marches, gracious sovereign, 140
Shall be a wall sufficient to defend
Our inland from the pilfering borderers.

KING

We do not mean the coursing snatchers only, 143
But fear the main intendment of the Scot, 144
Who hath been still a giddy neighbor to us; 145
For you shall read that my great-grandfather
Never went with his forces into France
But that the Scot on his unfurnished kingdom 148
Came pouring like the tide into a breach,
With ample and brim fullness of his force,
Galling the gleanèd land with hot assays, 151
Girding with grievous siege castles and towns;
That England, being empty of defense,
Hath shook and trembled at th' ill neighborhood. 154

CANTERBURY

She hath been then more feared than harmed, my liege; 155
For hear her but exampled by herself;
When all her chivalry hath been in France
And she a mourning widow of her nobles,
She hath herself not only well defended
But taken and impounded as a stray 160

137 *lay . . . proportions* estimate our forces 138 *road* inroads 139 *all advantages* every opportunity 140 *marches* i.e. northern borderlands 143 *coursing snatchers* mounted raiders 144 *intendment* intent, design 145 *still* always; *giddy* unstable 148 *unfurnished* unprepared 151 *gleanèd* stripped (of manpower) 154 *neighborhood* neighborliness 155 *feared* frightened 160 *as a stray* like a stray beast

The King of Scots; whom she did send to France
To fill King Edward's fame with prisoner kings,
And make her chronicle as rich with praise
164 As is the ooze and bottom of the sea
165 With sunken wrack and sumless treasuries.

ELY

But there's a saying very old and true:
'If that you will France win,
Then with Scotland first begin.'
For once the eagle England being in prey,
To her unguarded nest the weasel Scot
Comes sneaking, and so sucks her princely eggs,
Playing the mouse in absence of the cat,
173 To 'tame and havoc more than she can eat.

EXETER

It follows then, the cat must stay at home;
175 Yet that is but a crushed necessity,
Since we have locks to safeguard necessaries
177 And pretty traps to catch the petty thieves.
While that the armèd hand doth fight abroad,
179 Th' advisèd head defends itself at home;
180 For government, though high, and low, and lower,
181 Put into parts, doth keep in one consent,
182 Congreeing in a full and natural close
Like music.

CANTERBURY Therefore doth heaven divide
The state of man in divers functions,
Setting endeavor in continual motion;
186 To which is fixèd as an aim or butt
Obedience; for so work the honeybees,
Creatures that by a rule in nature teach
The act of order to a peopled kingdom.

164 *ooze and bottom* oozy bottom 165 *sumless* inestimable 173 *'tame* attame, broach 175 *crushed* voided 177 *pretty* neat 179 *advisèd* prudent 180–81 *though . . . parts* i.e. though made up of three estates 181 *one* mutual 182 *Congreeing* agreeing; *close* cadence 186 *fixèd as* attached like; *aim or butt* i.e. target

They have a king, and officers of sorts,
Where some like magistrates correct at home, 191
Others like merchants venture trade abroad,
Others like soldiers armèd in their stings
Make boot upon the summer's velvet buds, 194
Which pillage they with merry march bring home
To the tent-royal of their emperor,
Who, busied in his majesties, surveys 197
The singing masons building roofs of gold,
The civil citizens kneading up the honey,
The poor mechanic porters crowding in
Their heavy burdens at his narrow gate,
The sad-eyed justice with his surly hum 202
Delivering o'er to executors pale 203
The lazy yawning drone. I this infer,
That many things having full reference 205
To one consent may work contrariously, 206
As many arrows loosèd several ways 207
Come to one mark;
As many several ways meet in one town,
As many fresh streams meet in one salt sea,
As many lines close in the dial's centre;
So may a thousand actions, once afoot,
End in one purpose, and be all well borne
Without defeat. Therefore to France, my liege!
Divide your happy England into four,
Whereof take you one quarter into France,
And you withal shall make all Gallia shake. 217
If we, with thrice such powers left at home,
Cannot defend our own doors from the dog,
Let us be worried, and our nation lose
The name of hardiness and policy. 221

191 *correct* maintain discipline **194** *Make boot* prey **197** *majesties* royal functions **202** *sad-eyed* solemn-eyed **203** *executors* executioners **205–06** *reference ... consent* i.e. relationship to a single agreement **206** *contrariously* diversely **207** *loosèd ... ways* i.e. shot from different angles **217** *Gallia* France **221** *policy* statesmanship

KING

Call in the messengers sent from the Dauphin.
[Exeunt some Attendants.]
Now are we well resolved, and by God's help
And yours, the noble sinews of our power,
225 France being ours, we'll bend it to our awe
Or break it all to pieces. Or there we'll sit,
227 Ruling in large and ample empery
O'er France and all her almost kingly dukedoms,
Or lay these bones in an unworthy urn,
Tombless, with no remembrance over them.
Either our history shall with full mouth
Speak freely of our acts, or else our grave,
Like Turkish mute, shall have a tongueless mouth,
234 Not worshipped with a waxen epitaph.

Enter Ambassadors of France [attended].

Now are we well prepared to know the pleasure
Of our fair cousin Dauphin; for we hear
Your greeting is from him, not from the king.

AMBASSADOR

May't please your majesty to give us leave
Freely to render what we have in charge,
Or shall we sparingly show you far off
The Dauphin's meaning and our embassy?

KING

We are no tyrant, but a Christian king,
Unto whose grace our passion is as subject
As is our wretches fett'red in our prisons.
Therefore with frank and with uncurbèd plainness
Tell us the Dauphin's mind.

AMBASSADOR Thus then, in few:
Your highness, lately sending into France,
Did claim some certain dukedoms in the right
Of your great predecessor, King Edward the Third.

225 *our awe* awe of us 227 *empery* sovereignty 234 *with . . . epitaph* i.e. with even so much as a wax (as opposed to durable bronze) epitaph

In answer of which claim, the prince our master
Says that you savor too much of your youth,
And bids you be advised: There's naught in France 252
That can be with a nimble galliard won; 253
You cannot revel into dukedoms there.
He therefore sends you, meeter for your spirit,
This tun of treasure; and in lieu of this,
Desires you let the dukedoms that you claim
Hear no more of you. This the Dauphin speaks.

KING
What treasure, uncle?

EXETER
Tennis balls, my liege.

KING
We are glad the Dauphin is so pleasant with us.
His present and your pains we thank you for.
When we have matched our rackets to these balls,
We will in France, by God's grace, play a set
Shall strike his father's crown into the hazard. 264
Tell him he hath made a match with such a wrangler 265
That all the courts of France will be disturbed 266
With chases. And we understand him well, 267
How he comes o'er us with our wilder days, 268
Not measuring what use we made of them.
We never valued this poor seat of England,
And therefore, living hence, did give ourself 271
To barbarous license; as 'tis ever common
That men are merriest when they are from home.
But tell the Dauphin I will keep my state, 274
Be like a king, and show my sail of greatness
When I do rouse me in my throne of France. 276

252 *be advised* take counsel 253 *galliard* merry dance 264 *crown* (1) symbol of majesty, (2) wager-money; *hazard* (1) an aperture functioning like a goal in an Elizabethan type of tennis court, (2) jeopardy 265 *wrangler* opponent 266 *courts* (1) tennis courts, (2) royal courts 267 *chases* (1) unsuccessful attempts to return tennis ball on first bounce, (2) pursuits 268 *comes o'er* taunts 271 *hence* i.e. out of our proper realm (France) 274 *state* kingly decorum 276 *rouse me in* mount

For that I have laid by my majesty
And plodded like a man for working days,
But I will rise there with so full a glory
That I will dazzle all the eyes of France,
Yea, strike the Dauphin blind to look on us.
And tell the pleasant prince this mock of his
283 Hath turned his balls to gunstones, and his soul
284 Shall stand sore chargèd for the wasteful vengeance
That shall fly with them; for many a thousand widows
Shall this his mock mock out of their dear husbands,
Mock mothers from their sons, mock castles down;
And some are yet ungotten and unborn
That shall have cause to curse the Dauphin's scorn.
But this lies all within the will of God,
To whom I do appeal, and in whose name,
Tell you the Dauphin, I am coming on
To venge me as I may, and to put forth
My rightful hand in a well-hallowed cause.
So get you hence in peace. And tell the Dauphin
His jest will savor but of shallow wit
When thousands weep more than did laugh at it.
Convey them with safe conduct. Fare you well.
Exeunt Ambassadors.

EXETER
This was a merry message.

KING
We hope to make the sender blush at it.
Therefore, my lords, omit no happy hour
That may give furth'rance to our expedition;
For we have now no thought in us but France,
Save those to God, that run before our business.
305 Therefore let our proportions for these wars
Be soon collected, and all things thought upon
That may with reasonable swiftness add
308 More feathers to our wings; for, God before,

283 *gunstones* cannon balls 284 *sore chargèd* grievously accused 305 *proportions* required forces 308 *God before* i.e. God leading

We'll chide this Dauphin at his father's door.
Therefore let every man now task his thought
That this fair action may on foot be brought. *Exeunt.*

*

Flourish. Enter Chorus. II, Cho.

Now all the youth of England are on fire,
And silken dalliance in the wardrobe lies. 2
Now thrive the armorers, and honor's thought
Reigns solely in the breast of every man.
They sell the pasture now to buy the horse,
Following the mirror of all Christian kings 6
With wingèd heels, as English Mercuries. 7
For now sits Expectation in the air
And hides a sword, from hilts unto the point, 9
With crowns imperial, crowns, and coronets
Promised to Harry and his followers.
The French, advised by good intelligence
Of this most dreadful preparation,
Shake in their fear, and with pale policy 14
Seek to divert the English purposes.
O England! model to thy inward greatness, 16
Like little body with a mighty heart,
What mightst thou do that honor would thee do,
Were all thy children kind and natural! 19
But see, thy fault France hath in thee found out,
A nest of hollow bosoms, which he fills 21
With treacherous crowns; and three corrupted men –
One, Richard Earl of Cambridge, and the second,
Henry Lord Scroop of Masham, and the third,

310 *task* exercise

II, Cho. **2** *silken dalliance* pleasure garments of silk **6** *mirror* image, pattern **7** *Mercuries* (Mercury, messenger of the gods, was usually pictured wearing winged sandals) **9** *hides a sword* i.e. completely impaled with captured crowns **14** *pale policy* timorous intrigue **16** *model to* i.e. small visible replica of **19** *kind* loyal to kindred **21** *hollow bosoms* (1) hypocrites, (2) empty receptacles for money

Sir Thomas Grey, knight, of Northumberland –
26 Have, for the gilt of France (O guilt indeed!),
Confirmed conspiracy with fearful France,
And by their hands this grace of kings must die,
If hell and treason hold their promises,
Ere he take ship for France, and in Southampton.
31 Linger your patience on, and we'll digest
Th' abuse of distance, force a play.
The sum is paid, the traitors are agreed,
The king is set from London, and the scene
Is now transported, gentles, to Southampton.
There is the playhouse now, there must you sit,
And thence to France shall we convey you safe
And bring you back, charming the narrow seas
39 To give you gentle pass; for, if we may,
40 We'll not offend one stomach with our play.
41 But, till the king come forth, and not till then,
Unto Southampton do we shift our scene. *Exit.*

II, i *Enter Corporal Nym and Lieutenant Bardolph.*

BARDOLPH Well met, Corporal Nym.

NYM Good morrow, Lieutenant Bardolph.

3 BARDOLPH What, are Ancient Pistol and you friends yet?

NYM For my part, I care not. I say little; but when time shall serve, there shall be smiles – but that shall be as it may. I dare not fight, but I will wink and hold out mine iron. It is a simple one, but what though? It will toast cheese, and it will endure cold as another man's sword will – and there's an end.

BARDOLPH I will bestow a breakfast to make you friends,

26 *gilt* i.e. gold crowns 31–32 *digest . . . play* i.e. render intelligible the shifting scene and compress the action 39 *pass* passage 40 *offend . . . stomach* (1) make seasick, (2) displease 41 *But, till* i.e. only when (ll. 41–42 were apparently added to the original speech – cf. ll. 35–36 – when the following comic episode, still set in London, was interpolated)
II, i A London street 3 *Ancient* ensign, standardbearer

and we'll be all three sworn brothers to France. Let 't be so, good Corporal Nym.

NYM Faith, I will live so long as I may, that's the certain of it; and when I cannot live any longer, I will do as I may. That is my rest, that is the rendezvous of it.

BARDOLPH It is certain, corporal, that he is married to Nell Quickly, and certainly she did you wrong, for you were troth-plight to her.

NYM I cannot tell. Things must be as they may. Men may sleep, and they may have their throats about them at that time, and some say knives have edges. It must be as it may. Though patience be a tired mare, yet she will plod. There must be conclusions. Well, I cannot tell.

Enter Pistol and [Hostess] Quickly.

BARDOLPH Here comes Ancient Pistol and his wife. Good corporal, be patient here.

NYM How now, mine host Pistol?

PISTOL
Base tyke, call'st thou me host?
Now by this hand I swear I scorn the term;
Nor shall my Nell keep lodgers!

HOSTESS No, by my troth, not long; for we cannot lodge and board a dozen or fourteen gentlewomen that live honestly by the prick of their needles but it will be thought we keep a bawdy house straight. *[Nym and Pistol draw.]* O well-a-day, Lady, if he be not hewn now, we shall see willful adultery and murder committed.

BARDOLPH Good lieutenant – good corporal – offer nothing here.

NYM Pish!

PISTOL Pish for thee, Iceland dog, thou prick-eared cur of Iceland!

15 *rest* last stake (in the game of primero); *rendezvous* resort 18 *troth-plight* betrothed 23 *conclusions* i.e. an end to everything 34 *if . . . hewn* i.e. if Nym is not cut down (?) 35 *adultery* (malapropism, for 'battery'?) 36–37 *offer nothing* i.e. do not offer to fight 39 *Iceland dog* (a breed with long hair and pointed ears)

HOSTESS Good Corporal Nym, show thy valor, and put up your sword.

NYM Will you shog off? I would have you solus.

PISTOL

'Solus,' egregious dog? O viper vile!
The 'solus' in thy most mervailous face!
The 'solus' in thy teeth, and in thy throat,
And in thy hateful lungs, yea, in thy maw, perdy!
And, which is worse, within thy nasty mouth!
I do retort the 'solus' in thy bowels;
For I can take, and Pistol's cock is up.
And flashing fire will follow.

NYM I am not Barbason; you cannot conjure me. I have an humor to knock you indifferently well. If you grow foul with me, Pistol, I will scour you with my rapier, as I may, in fair terms. If you would walk off, I would prick your guts a little in good terms, as I may, and that's the humor of it.

PISTOL

O braggard vile, and damnèd furious wight,
The grave doth gape, and doting death is near.
Therefore exhale!

BARDOLPH Hear me, hear me what I say! He that strikes the first stroke, I'll run him up to the hilts, as I am a soldier. *[Draws.]*

PISTOL

An oath of mickle might, and fury shall abate.
[Pistol and Nym sheathe their swords.]
Give me thy fist, thy forefoot to me give.
Thy spirits are most tall.

43 *shog off* move along; *solus* alone (taken by Pistol as an insult) 45 *mervailous* marvellous (?) 47 *maw* belly; *perdy* (mild oath, from '*par dieu*') 48 *nasty* foul-speaking 50 *take* strike; *cock is up* i.e. anger is aroused (with play on 'cocked Pistol') 52 *Barbason* (name of a devil, Pistol's preceding speech having resembled a formula for exorcising devils) 53 *foul* (from firing) 54 *rapier* (serving as a scouring-rod) 56–57 *that's . . . it* i.e. that's my mood (an all-purpose tag, glancing at popular abuse of the terms of 'humoral' psychology) 60 *exhale* expire

NYM I will cut thy throat one time or other in fair terms. That is the humor of it.

PISTOL

Coupe la gorge!
That is the word. I thee defy again.
O hound of Crete, think'st thou my spouse to get?
No; to the spital go,
And from the powd'ring tub of infamy
Fetch forth the lazar kite of Cressid's kind,
Doll Tearsheet, she by name, and her espouse.
I have, and I will hold, the quondam Quickly
For the only she; and, pauca! there's enough.
Go to!

Enter the Boy.

BOY Mine host Pistol, you must come to my master – and you, hostess. He is very sick and would to bed. Good Bardolph, put thy face between his sheets and do the office of a warming pan. Faith, he's very ill.

BARDOLPH Away, you rogue!

HOSTESS By my troth, he'll yield the crow a pudding one of these days. The king has killed his heart. Good husband, come home presently. *Exit.*

BARDOLPH Come, shall I make you two friends? We must to France together: why the devil should we keep knives to cut one another's throats?

PISTOL

Let floods o'erswell and fiends for food howl on!

NYM You'll pay me the eight shillings I won of you at betting?

PISTOL

Base is the slave that pays.

NYM That now I will have. That's the humor of it.

68 *Coupe la gorge* cut the throat 70 *hound of Crete* (a shaggy breed) 71 *spital* hospital 72 *powd'ring tub* sweating tub (used as cure for venereal disease) 73 *lazar kite* leprous bird of prey; *Cressid's kind* i.e. prostitute (a popular epithet, derived from Cressida's fate in Henryson's *Testament*) 76 *pauca* i.e. in few words 83 *yield . . . pudding* i.e. become carrion food 85 *presently* at once

PISTOL
As manhood shall compound. Push home.
[They] draw.

BARDOLPH By this sword, he that makes the first thrust, I'll kill him! By this sword, I will.
[Draws.]

PISTOL
'Sword' is an oath, and oaths must have their course.
[Sheathes his sword.]

BARDOLPH Corporal Nym, an thou wilt be friends, be friends; an thou wilt not, why then be enemies with me too. Prithee put up.

[NYM I shall have my eight shillings I won of you at betting?]

PISTOI
A noble shalt thou have, and present pay;
And liquor likewise will I give to thee,
And friendship shall combine, and brotherhood.
I'll live by Nym, and Nym shall live by me.
Is not this just? For I shall sutler be
Unto the camp, and profits will accrue.
Give me thy hand.
[Nym sheathes his sword.]

NYM I shall have my noble?

PISTOL
In cash, most justly paid.

NYM Well then, that's the humor of't.
Enter Hostess.

HOSTESS As ever you come of women, come in quickly to Sir John. Ah, poor heart! he is so shaked of a burning quotidian tertian that it is most lamentable to behold. Sweet men, come to him.

NYM The king hath run bad humors on the knight; that's the even of it.

94 *compound* settle it 103 *noble* 6s. 8d. (in cash) 113 *come* are born 115 *quotidian tertian* (confusion of 'tertian' fever, which occurs on alternate days, with 'quotidian,' which occurs daily) 118 *the even of it* i.e. on the level

PISTOL
Nym, thou hast spoke the right.
His heart is fracted and corroborate.
NYM The king is a good king, but it must be as it may:
he passes some humors and careers. 122
PISTOL
Let us condole the knight; for, lambkins, we will live.
[Exeunt.]

*

Enter Exeter, Bedford, and Westmoreland. II, ii
BEDFORD
'Fore God, his grace is bold to trust these traitors.
EXETER
They shall be apprehended by and by.
WESTMORELAND
How smooth and even they do bear themselves,
As if allegiance in their bosoms sat
Crownèd with faith and constant loyalty!
BEDFORD
The king hath note of all that they intend
By interception which they dream not of.
EXETER
Nay, but the man that was his bedfellow, 8
Whom he hath dulled and cloyed with gracious favors – 9
That he should, for a foreign purse, so sell
His sovereign's life to death and treachery!
Sound trumpets. Enter the King, Scroop, Cambridge, and Grey [, Lords, and Attendants].
KING
Now sits the wind fair, and we will aboard.
My Lord of Cambridge, and my kind Lord of Masham,
And you, my gentle knight, give me your thoughts.

120 *fracted* broken; *corroborate* pieced together by grace, reconciled (probably a malapropism) 122 *passes* indulges in; *careers* capers
II, ii The King's quarters at Southampton 8 *bedfellow* favorite (Scroop)
9 *cloyed* surfeited

Think you not that the pow'rs we bear with us
Will cut their passage through the force of France,
Doing the execution and the act
For which we have in head assembled them?

SCROOP
No doubt, my liege, if each man do his best.

KING
I doubt not that, since we are well persuaded
We carry not a heart with us from hence
That grows not in a fair consent with ours,
Nor leave not one behind that doth not wish
Success and conquest to attend on us.

CAMBRIDGE
Never was monarch better feared and loved
Than is your majesty. There's not, I think, a subject
That sits in heart-grief and uneasiness
Under the sweet shade of your government.

GREY
True. Those that were your father's enemies
Have steeped their galls in honey and do serve you
With hearts create of duty and of zeal.

KING
We therefore have great cause of thankfulness,
And shall forget the office of our hand
Sooner than quittance of desert and merit
According to the weight and worthiness.

SCROOP
So service shall with steelèd sinews toil,
And labor shall refresh itself with hope,
To do your grace incessant services.

KING
We judge no less. Uncle of Exeter,
Enlarge the man committed yesterday
That railed against our person. We consider
It was excess of wine that set him on,

18 *head* an army 30 *galls* sources of bitterness 33 *office* use 34 *quittance* requital 40 *Enlarge* set free

And on his more advice, we pardon him. 43

SCROOP

That's mercy, but too much security: 44
Let him be punished, sovereign, lest example
Breed by his sufferance more of such a kind. 46

KING

O, let us yet be merciful.

CAMBRIDGE

So may your highness, and yet punish too.

GREY

Sir,
You show great mercy if you give him life
After the taste of much correction.

KING

Alas, your too much love and care of me
Are heavy orisons 'gainst this poor wretch. 53
If little faults proceeding on distemper 54
Shall not be winked at, how shall we stretch our eye
When capital crimes, chewed, swallowed, and digested, 56
Appear before us? We'll yet enlarge that man,
Though Cambridge, Scroop, and Grey, in their dear care
And tender preservation of our person,
Would have him punished. And now to our French causes.
Who are the late commissioners? 61

CAMBRIDGE

I one, my lord.
Your highness bade me ask for it to-day. 63

SCROOP

So did you me, my liege.

GREY

And I, my royal sovereign.

43 *more advice* i.e. recovered judgment 44 *security* overconfidence 46 *his sufferance* toleration of him 53 *Are heavy orisons* i.e. beget weighty pleas 54 *proceeding on distemper* following drunkenness 56 *chewed . . . digested* i.e. premeditated 61 *late* lately appointed 63 *it* i.e. the commission

KING

Then, Richard Earl of Cambridge, there is yours;
There yours, Lord Scroop of Masham; and, sir knight,
Grey of Northumberland, this same is yours.
Read them, and know I know your worthiness.
My Lord of Westmoreland, and uncle Exeter,
We will aboard to-night. – Why, how now, gentlemen?
What see you in those papers that you lose
So much complexion? – Look ye, how they change!
Their cheeks are paper. – Why, what read you there
75 That hath so cowarded and chased your blood
76 Out of appearance?

CAMBRIDGE I do confess my fault,
And do submit me to your highness' mercy.

GREY, SCROOP

To which we all appeal.

KING

79 The mercy that was quick in us but late,
By your own counsel is suppressed and killed.
You must not dare for shame to talk of mercy;
82 For your own reasons turn into your bosoms
As dogs upon their masters, worrying you.
See you, my princes and my noble peers,
85 These English monsters! My Lord of Cambridge here –
86 You know how apt our love was to accord
87 To furnish him with all appertinents
Belonging to his honor; and this man
Hath, for a few light crowns, lightly conspired
90 And sworn unto the practices of France
To kill us here in Hampton; to the which
This knight, no less for bounty bound to us
Than Cambridge is, hath likewise sworn. But O,
What shall I say to thee, Lord Scroop, thou cruel,

75 *cowarded* frightened 76 *appearance* sight 79 *quick* living 82 *turn* return 85 *English monsters* (as distinct from exotic freaks imported for exhibition) 86 *accord* consent 87 *appertinents* appurtenances 90 *practices* plots

Ingrateful, savage, and inhuman creature?
Thou that didst bear the key of all my counsels,
That knew'st the very bottom of my soul,
That almost mightst have coined me into gold,
Wouldst thou have practiced on me for thy use?
May it be possible that foreign hire
Could out of thee extract one spark of evil
That might annoy my finger? 'Tis so strange 102
That, though the truth of it stands off as gross
As black and white, my eye will scarcely see it.
Treason and murder ever kept together,
As two yoke-devils sworn to either's purpose,
Working so grossly in a natural cause 107
That admiration did not whoop at them;
But thou, 'gainst all proportion, didst bring in 109
Wonder to wait on treason and on murder; 110
And whatsoever cunning fiend it was
That wrought upon thee so preposterously 112
Hath got the voice in hell for excellence. 113
All other devils that suggest by treasons 114
Do botch and bungle up damnation 115
With patches, colors, and with forms being fetched
From glist'ring semblances of piety;
But he that tempered thee bade thee stand up, 118
Gave thee no instance why thou shouldst do treason,
Unless to dub thee with the name of traitor. 120
If that same demon that hath gulled thee thus
Should with his lion gait walk the whole world,
He might return to vasty Tartar back 123
And tell the legions, 'I can never win
A soul so easy as that Englishman's.'

102 *annoy* injure 107–08 *Working . . . them* i.e. cooperating with such obvious fitness as to provoke no cry of wonder 109 *proportion* fitness 110 *wait on* attend 112 *preposterously* abnormally 113 *voice* vote; *excellence* supreme achievement 114 *suggest* tempt 115–17 *Do botch . . . piety* i.e. trick out sin with disguises of shining virtue 118 *tempered* moulded; *stand up* volunteer 120 *dub . . . name* acquire the title 123 *Tartar* Tartarus (deepest Hades)

126 O, how hast thou with jealousy infected
127 The sweetness of affiance! Show men dutiful?
Why, so didst thou. Seem they grave and learnèd?
Why, so didst thou. Come they of noble family?
Why, so didst thou. Seem they religious?
Why, so didst thou. Or are they spare in diet,
Free from gross passion or of mirth or anger,
133 Constant in spirit, not swerving with the blood,
134 Garnished and decked in modest complement,
135 Not working with the eye without the ear,
And but in purgèd judgment trusting neither?
137 Such and so finely bolted didst thou seem;
And thus thy fall hath left a kind of blot
139 To mark the full-fraught man and best indued
With some suspicion. I will weep for thee;
For this revolt of thine, methinks, is like
Another fall of man. Their faults are open.
Arrest them to the answer of the law;
And God acquit them of their practices!

EXETER I arrest thee of high treason by the name of Richard Earl of Cambridge.

I arrest thee of high treason by the name of Henry Lord Scroop of Masham.

I arrest thee of high treason by the name of Thomas Grey, knight, of Northumberland.

SCROOP
Our purposes God justly hath discovered,
And I repent my faults more than my death,
Which I beseech your highness to forgive,
Although my body pay the price of it.

CAMBRIDGE
For me, the gold of France did not seduce,

126 *jealousy* suspicion 127 *affiance* trust 133 *blood* passions 134 *decked . . . complement* i.e. wearing the look of modesty 135–36 *Not . . . neither* i.e. judiciously trusting neither eye nor ear alone 137 *bolted* sifted, refined 139 *full-fraught* most richly endowed

Although I did admit it as a motive 156
The sooner to effect what I intended.
But God be thankèd for prevention,
Which I in sufferance heartily will rejoice, 159
Beseeching God, and you, to pardon me.

GREY

Never did faithful subject more rejoice
At the discovery of most dangerous treason
Than I do at this hour joy o'er myself,
Prevented from a damnèd enterprise.
My fault, but not my body, pardon, sovereign.

KING

God quit you in his mercy! Hear your sentence. 166
You have conspired against our royal person,
Joined with an enemy proclaimed, and from his coffers
Received the golden earnest of our death; 169
Wherein you would have sold your king to slaughter,
His princes and his peers to servitude,
His subjects to oppression and contempt,
And his whole kingdom into desolation.
Touching our person, seek we no revenge,
But we our kingdom's safety must so tender, 175
Whose ruin you have sought, that to her laws
We do deliver you. Get you therefore hence,
Poor miserable wretches, to your death;
The taste whereof God of his mercy give
You patience to endure and true repentance
Of all your dear offenses! Bear them hence. 181
Exit [Guard, with Cambridge, Scroop, and Grey].
Now, lords, for France; the enterprise whereof
Shall be to you as us, like glorious. 183
We doubt not of a fair and lucky war,

156 *did admit* allowed to stand (the actual 'motive' of Cambridge, here scarcely glanced at, was to further Mortimer's claim to the crown) 159 *sufferance* suffering 166 *quit* acquit, forgive 169 *earnest* advance payment 175 *tender* hold dear 181 *dear* rare 183 *like* alike

Since God so graciously hath brought to light
This dangerous treason, lurking in our way
To hinder our beginnings. We doubt not now
188 But every rub is smoothèd on our way.
Then forth, dear countrymen. Let us deliver
Our puissance into the hand of God,
191 Putting it straight in expedition.
192 Cheerly to sea the signs of war advance.
No king of England, if not King of France!

Flourish. [Exeunt.]

*

II, iii *Enter Pistol, Nym, Bardolph, Boy, and Hostess.*

HOSTESS Prithee, honey-sweet husband, let me bring
2 thee to Staines.

PISTOL
3 No; for my manly heart doth earn.
Bardolph, be blithe; Nym, rouse thy vaunting veins;
Boy, bristle thy courage up; for Falstaff he is dead,
6 And we must earn therefore.

BARDOLPH Would I were with him, wheresome'er he is,
either in heaven or in hell!

9 HOSTESS Nay sure, he's not in hell! He's in Arthur's
bosom, if ever man went to Arthur's bosom. 'A made a
11 finer end, and went away an it had been any christom
child. 'A parted ev'n just between twelve and one, ev'n
at the turning o' th' tide. For after I saw him fumble with
the sheets, and play with flowers, and smile upon his
finger's end, I knew there was but one way; for his nose
16 was as sharp as a pen, and 'a babbled of green fields.

188 *But* but that; *rub* obstacle (bowling term) 191 *expedition* motion
192 *signs* ensigns

II, iii A London street 2 *Staines* place on the road to Southampton 3, 6 *earn* grieve 9 *Arthur* (confused with Abraham) 11 *christom* newly baptized 16 *'a . . . fields* (authenticating this famous emendation is the likelihood that the Hostess, whose religious education is defective – cf. *Arthur's bosom* – has been puzzled by 'green pastures' as Falstaff repeated the 23rd Psalm)

'How now, Sir John?' quoth I. 'What, man? be o' good cheer.' So 'a cried out 'God, God, God!' three or four times. Now I, to comfort him, bid him 'a should not think of God; I hoped there was no need to trouble himself with any such thoughts yet. So 'a bade me lay more clothes on his feet. I put my hand into the bed and felt them, and they were as cold as any stone. Then I felt to his knees, and so upward and upward, and all was as cold as any stone.

NYM They say he cried out of sack.

HOSTESS Ay, that 'a did.

BARDOLPH And of women.

HOSTESS Nay, that 'a did not.

BOY Yes, that 'a did, and said they were devils incarnate.

HOSTESS 'A could never abide carnation; 'twas a color he never liked.

BOY 'A said once the devil would have him about women.

HOSTESS 'A did in some sort, indeed, handle women; but then he was rheumatic, and talked of the Whore of Babylon.

BOY Do you not remember 'a saw a flea stick upon Bardolph's nose, and 'a said it was a black soul burning in hell?

BARDOLPH Well, the fuel is gone that maintained that fire. That's all the riches I got in his service.

NYM Shall we shog? The king will be gone from Southampton.

PISTOL

Come, let's away. My love, give me thy lips.
Look to my chattels and my moveables.
Let senses rule. The word is 'Pitch and pay.'
Trust none;

25 *cried . . . sack* exclaimed against wine 34 *rheumatic* i.e. feverish (with pronunciation 'rom-atic' triggering the allusion to 'Whore of Babylon,' i.e. the Roman Church) 38 *fuel* i.e. liquor supplied by Falstaff 40 *shog* move along 44 *Let . . . rule* i.e. use your eyes and ears; *Pitch and pay* i.e. cash down

46 For oaths are straws, men's faiths are wafer-cakes,
47 And Hold-fast is the only dog, my duck.
48 Therefore Caveto be thy counsellor.
49 Go, clear thy crystals. Yoke-fellows in arms,
Let us to France, like horse-leeches, my boys,
To suck, to suck, the very blood to suck!

BOY And that's but unwholesome food, they say.

PISTOL
Touch her soft mouth, and march.

BARDOLPH Farewell, hostess.
[Kisses her.]

NYM I cannot kiss, that is the humor of it; but adieu!

PISTOL
56 Let housewifery appear. Keep close, I thee command.

HOSTESS Farewell, adieu! *Exeunt.*

*

II, iv *Flourish. Enter the French King, the Dauphin, the Dukes of Berri and Britaine [, the Constable, and others].*

KING
Thus comes the English with full power upon us,
And more than carefully it us concerns
To answer royally in our defenses.
Therefore the Dukes of Berri and Britaine,
Of Brabant and of Orleans, shall make forth,
And you, Prince Dauphin, with all swift dispatch,
7 To line and new repair our towns of war
With men of courage and with means defendant;
For England his approaches makes as fierce
As waters to the sucking of a gulf.

46 *wafer-cakes* i.e. easily broken (proverbial) 47 *Hold-fast . . . dog* (from proverb, 'Brag is a good dog, but Hold-fast is a better') 48 *Caveto* beware 49 *clear thy crystals* i.e. wipe your eyes 56 *Let . . . appear* i.e. be a good housekeeper; *close* i.e. indoors

II, iv Within the palace of the French King 7 *line* reinforce 10 *sucking* i.e. whirlpool

It fits us then to be as provident
As fear may teach us out of late examples 12
Left by the fatal and neglected English 13
Upon our fields.
DAUPHIN My most redoubted father,
It is most meet we arm us 'gainst the foe; 15
For peace itself should not so dull a kingdom
Though war nor no known quarrel were in question
But that defenses, musters, preparations
Should be maintained, assembled, and collected,
As were a war in expectation.
Therefore I say 'tis meet we all go forth
To view the sick and feeble parts of France;
And let us do it with no show of fear –
No, with no more than if we heard that England
Were busied with a Whitsun morris dance; 25
For, my good liege, she is so idly kinged, 26
Her sceptre so fantastically borne,
By a vain, giddy, shallow, humorous youth,
That fear attends her not. 29
CONSTABLE O peace, Prince Dauphin!
You are too much mistaken in this king.
Question your grace the late ambassadors,
With what great state he heard their embassy,
How well supplied with noble counsellors,
How modest in exception, and withal 34
How terrible in constant resolution,
And you shall find his vanities forespent 36
Were but the outside of the Roman Brutus, 37
Covering discretion with a coat of folly;
As gardeners do with ordure hide those roots
That shall first spring and be most delicate.

12 *examples* i.e. of military defeats **13** *fatal and neglected* fatally disregarded **15** *meet* fitting **25** *Whitsun* festal week beginning the seventh Sunday after Easter; *morris dance* folk dance in antic costumes **26** *idly* worthlessly **29** *attends* accompanies **34** *exception* taking issue **36** *forespent* now done with **37** *Brutus* Lucius Junius Brutus, who disguised his acumen from the tyrant Tarquin Superbus until ready to join in revolt

DAUPHIN
Well, 'tis not so, my Lord High Constable!
But though we think it so, it is no matter.
In cases of defense 'tis best to weigh
The enemy more mighty than he seems.
So the proportions of defense are filled;
Which of a weak and niggardly projection
Doth, like a miser, spoil his coat with scanting
A little cloth.

KING Think we King Harry strong;
And, princes, look you strongly arm to meet him.
The kindred of him hath been fleshed upon us;
And he is bred out of that bloody strain
That haunted us in our familiar paths.
Witness our too much memorable shame
When Crécy battle fatally was struck,
And all our princes captived, by the hand
Of that black name, Edward, Black Prince of Wales;
Whiles that his mountain sire – on mountain standing,
Up in the air, crowned with the golden sun –
Saw his heroical seed, and smiled to see him
Mangle the work of nature, and deface
The patterns that by God and by French fathers
Had twenty years been made. This is a stem
Of that victorious stock; and let us fear
The native mightiness and fate of him.

Enter a Messenger.

MESSENGER
Ambassadors from Harry King of England
Do crave admittance to your majesty.

KING
We'll give them present audience. Go, and bring them.
[Exeunt Messenger and certain Lords.]

45 *proportions* adequate forces 46–47 *Which . . . Doth* (grammatically incoherent, possibly owing to a missing line, but clear in sense) 46 *weak . . . projection* small and miserly scale 50 *fleshed* initiated in blood shedding 54 *struck* waged 57 *mountain* i.e. towering (?) 64 *fate* fortune, luck

You see this chase is hotly followed, friends.
DAUPHIN
Turn head, and stop pursuit; for coward dogs 69
Most spend their mouths when what they seem to threaten
Runs far before them. Good my sovereign,
Take up the English short and let them know
Of what a monarchy you are the head.
Self-love, my liege, is not so vile a sin
As self-neglecting.
Enter [Lords, with] Exeter [and Train].
KING From our brother of England?
EXETER
From him, and thus he greets your majesty:
He wills you, in the name of God Almighty,
That you divest yourself, and lay apart
The borrowed glories that by gift of heaven,
By law of nature and of nations, 'longs 80
To him and to his heirs – namely, the crown
And all wide-stretchèd honors that pertain 82
By custom, and the ordinance of times, 83
Unto the crown of France. That you may know
'Tis no sinister nor no awkward claim, 85
Picked from the wormholes of long-vanished days,
Nor from the dust of old oblivion raked,
He sends you this most memorable line, 88
[Gives a paper.]
In every branch truly demonstrative;
Willing you overlook this pedigree;
And when you find him evenly derived 91
From his most famed of famous ancestors,
Edward the Third, he bids you then resign

69 *Turn head* stand at bay; *stop* i.e. put an end to 80 *By law . . . nations* i.e. morally and legally; *'longs* belongs 82 *all wide-stretchèd* i.e. the whole range of 83 *ordinance of times* decree of tradition 85 *sinister* illegitimate; *awkward* shambling 88 *line* line of descent 91 *evenly* directly

94 Your crown and kingdom, indirectly held
95 From him, the native and true challenger.

KING

Or else what follows?

EXETER

97 Bloody constraint; for if you hide the crown
Even in your hearts, there will he rake for it.
Therefore in fierce tempest is he coming,
In thunder and in earthquake, like a Jove;
101 That if requiring fail, he will compel;
102 And bids you, in the bowels of the Lord,
Deliver up the crown, and to take mercy
On the poor souls for whom this hungry war
Opens his vasty jaws; and on your head
106 Turning the widows' tears, the orphans' cries,
107 The dead men's blood, the privèd maidens' groans,
For husbands, fathers, and betrothèd lovers
That shall be swallowed in this controversy.
This is his claim, his threat'ning, and my message;
Unless the Dauphin be in presence here,
To whom expressly I bring greeting too.

KING

For us, we will consider of this further.
To-morrow shall you bear our full intent
Back to our brother of England.

DAUPHIN For the Dauphin,
I stand here for him. What to him from England?

EXETER

Scorn and defiance, slight regard, contempt,
And anything that may not misbecome
The mighty sender, doth he prize you at.
Thus says my king: and if your father's highness
Do not, in grant of all demands at large,

94 *indirectly* wrongfully **95** *challenger* claimant **97** *constraint* force **101** *requiring* demanding **102** *in the bowels* i.e. in the very being (Biblical metaphor) **106** *Turning* retorting, flinging back **107** *privèd* deprived (i.e. of their *betrothèd lovers*)

Sweeten the bitter mock you sent his majesty,
He'll call you to so hot an answer of it
That caves and womby vaultages of France
Shall chide your trespass, and return your mock
In second accent of his ordinance.

DAUPHIN

Say, if my father render fair return,
It is against my will; for I desire
Nothing but odds with England. To that end,
As matching to his youth and vanity,
I did present him with the Paris balls.

EXETER

He'll make your Paris Louvre shake for it,
Were it the mistress court of mighty Europe;
And be assured you'll find a difference,
As we his subjects have in wonder found,
Between the promise of his greener days
And these he masters now. Now he weighs time
Even to the utmost grain. That you shall read
In your own losses, if he stay in France.

KING

To-morrow shall you know our mind at full.
Flourish.

EXETER

Dispatch us with all speed, lest that our king
Come here himself to question our delay;
For he is footed in this land already.

KING

You shall be soon dispatched with fair conditions.
A night is but small breath and little pause
To answer matters of this consequence. *Exeunt.*

*

124 *womby vaultages* hollow caverns 126 *second accent* i.e. echo; *ordinance* cannon 131 *Paris balls* tennis balls 132 *Louvre* (pronounced 'lover' with play on *mistress* in next line) 137 *masters* governs

III, Cho. *Enter Chorus.*

1 Thus with imagined wing our swift scene flies,
In motion of no less celerity
Than that of thought. Suppose that you have seen
The well-appointed king at Hampton pier
Embark his royalty; and his brave fleet
6 With silken streamers the young Phoebus fanning.
Play with your fancies, and in them behold
Upon the hempen tackle shipboys climbing;
Hear the shrill whistle which doth order give
10 To sounds confused; behold the threaden sails,
Borne with th' invisible and creeping wind,
12 Draw the huge bottoms through the furrowed sea,
Breasting the lofty surge. O, do but think
14 You stand upon the rivage and behold
A city on th' inconstant billows dancing;
For so appears this fleet majestical,
Holding due course to Harfleur. Follow, follow!
18 Grapple your minds to sternage of this navy,
And leave your England as dead midnight still,
Guarded with grandsires, babies, and old women,
21 Either past or not arrived to pith and puissance;
For who is he whose chin is but enriched
With one appearing hair that will not follow
These culled and choice-drawn cavaliers to France?
Work, work your thoughts, and therein see a siege:
Behold the ordinance on their carriages,
27 With fatal mouths gaping on girded Harfleur.
Suppose th' ambassador from the French comes back;
Tells Harry that the king doth offer him
Katherine his daughter, and with her to dowry
Some petty and unprofitable dukedoms.

III, Cho. 1 *imagined wing* wing of imagination 6 *the . . . fanning* i.e. waving in the dawn 10 *threaden* woven of thread 12 *bottoms* hulls 14 *rivage* shore 18 *Grapple* fasten; *sternage* the wake 21 *pith* muscle, strength 27 *girded* surrounded, besieged

The offer likes not; and the nimble gunner
With linstock now the devilish cannon touches,
Alarum, and chambers go off.
And down goes all before them. Still be kind,
And eke out our performance with your mind. *Exit.*

Enter the King, Exeter, Bedford, and Gloucester. Alarum: [with Soldiers carrying] scaling ladders at Harfleur. III, i

KING
Once more unto the breach, dear friends, once more,
Or close the wall up with our English dead!
In peace there's nothing so becomes a man
As modest stillness and humility,
But when the blast of war blows in our ears,
Then imitate the action of the tiger:
Stiffen the sinews, summon up the blood,
Disguise fair nature with hard-favored rage;
Then lend the eye a terrible aspect:
Let it pry through the portage of the head
Like the brass cannon; let the brow o'erwhelm it
As fearfully as doth a gallèd rock
O'erhang and jutty his confounded base,
Swilled with the wild and wasteful ocean.
Now set the teeth and stretch the nostril wide,
Hold hard the breath and bend up every spirit
To his full height! On, on, you noble English,
Whose blood is fet from fathers of war-proof,
Fathers that like so many Alexanders
Have in these parts from morn till even fought

32 *likes* pleases 33 *linstock* lighting-stick
III, i Before the walls of Harfleur 10 *portage* portholes 12 *gallèd* eroded (at base) 13 *jutty his confounded* jut over its ruined 14 *Swilled* consumed 18 *fet* fetched, derived

21 And sheathed their swords for lack of argument.
Dishonor not your mothers; now attest
That those whom you called fathers did beget you!
24 Be copy now to men of grosser blood
And teach them how to war! And you, good yeomen,
Whose limbs were made in England, show us here
27 The mettle of your pasture. Let us swear
That you are worth your breeding; which I doubt not,
For there is none of you so mean and base
That hath not noble lustre in your eyes.
31 I see you stand like greyhounds in the slips,
Straining upon the start. The game 's afoot!
Follow your spirit; and upon this charge
34 Cry 'God for Harry! England and Saint George!'

[Exeunt.] Alarum, and chambers go off.

III, ii *Enter Nym, Bardolph, Pistol, and Boy.*

BARDOLPH On, on, on, on, on! to the breach, to the breach!

2 NYM Pray thee, corporal, stay. The knocks are too hot;
3 and, for mine own part, I have not a case of lives. The
4 humor of it is too hot; that is the very plain-song of it.

PISTOL
The plain-song is most just; for humors do abound.
Knocks go and come; God's vassals drop and die;
And sword and shield
In bloody field
Doth win immortal fame.

BOY Would I were in an alehouse in London! I would give all my fame for a pot of ale and safety.

PISTOL And I:
If wishes would prevail with me,
My purpose should not fail with me,
But thither would I hie.

21 *argument* opposition **24** *copy* examples **27** *mettle . . . pasture* quality of your rearing **31** *slips* leashes **34** *Saint George* (England's patron saint)
III, ii 2 *corporal* (at II, i, 2 Bardolph was a lieutenant) **3** *case* set **4** *plain-song* unelaborated melody, i.e. unadorned truth

BOY As duly, but not as truly,
As bird doth sing on bough.

Enter Fluellen.

FLUELLEN Up to the preach, you dogs! Avaunt, you cul- 18
lions!

[Drives them in.]

PISTOL
Be merciful, great duke, to men of mould! 19
Abate thy rage, abate thy manly rage,
Abate thy rage, great duke!
Good bawcock, bate thy rage! Use lenity, sweet chuck! 22

NYM These be good humors. Your honor wins bad hu- 23
mors. *Exit [with all but Boy].*

BOY As young as I am, I have observed these three swash- 25
ers. I am boy to them all three; but all they three, though
they would serve me, could not be man to me; for indeed
three such antics do not amount to a man. For Bardolph, 28
he is white-livered and red-faced; by the means whereof
'a faces it out, but fights not. For Pistol, he hath a killing
tongue and a quiet sword; by the means whereof 'a
breaks words and keeps whole weapons. For Nym, he 32
hath heard that men of few words are the best men, and
therefore he scorns to say his prayers, lest 'a should be
thought a coward; but his few bad words are matched
with as few good deeds, for 'a never broke any man's
head but his own, and that was against a post when he
was drunk. They will steal anything, and call it purchase.
Bardolph stole a lute-case, bore it twelve leagues, and
sold it for three halfpence. Nym and Bardolph are sworn
brothers in filching, and in Calais they stole a fire-shovel.
I knew by that piece of service the men would carry coals. 42
They would have me as familiar with men's pockets as

18 *Avaunt* be gone; *cullions* base fellows 19 *men of mould* mere mortals 22 *bawcock* fine fellow (from '*beau coq*') 23–24 *These . . . humors* (a cryptic utterance, even for Nym) 25 *swashers* swashbucklers 28 *antics* fantastics, zanies 32 *breaks* i.e. fails to keep his 42 *carry coals* i.e. put up with abuse

44 their gloves or their handkerchers; which makes much
against my manhood, if I should take from another's pocket to put into mine; for it is plain pocketing up of wrongs. I must leave them and seek some better service. Their villainy goes against my weak stomach, and therefore I must cast it up. *Exit.*

Enter Gower [and Fluellen].

GOWER Captain Fluellen, you must come presently to the mines. The Duke of Gloucester would speak with you.

FLUELLEN To the mines? Tell you the duke, it is not so
53 good to come to the mines; for look you, the mines is not
54 according to the disciplines of the war. The concavities
of it is not sufficient; for look you, th' athversary, you
56 may discuss unto the duke, look you, is digt himself four
57 yard under the countermines. By Cheshu, I think 'a will
58 plow up all, if there is not petter directions.

GOWER The Duke of Gloucester, to whom the order of the siege is given, is altogether directed by an Irishman, a very valiant gentleman, i' faith.

FLUELLEN It is Captain Macmorris, is it not?

GOWER I think it be.

FLUELLEN By Cheshu, he is an ass as in the orld! I will
65 verify as much in his peard. He has no more directions
in the true disciplines of the wars, look you, of the Roman disciplines, than is a puppy-dog.

Enter Macmorris and Captain Jamy.

GOWER Here 'a comes, and the Scots captain, Captain Jamy, with him.

FLUELLEN Captain Jamy is a marvellous falorous gentle-
71 man, that is certain, and of great expedition and know-
ledge in th' aunchient wars, upon my particular knowledge of his directions. By Cheshu, he will main-

44 *makes* i.e. offends 53 *mines* undermining operations 54 *disciplines* i.e. correct procedure; *concavities* i.e. slope, downward pitch 56 *discuss* explain 57 *Cheshu* Jesu 58 *plow* blow 65 *in his peard* in his beard, i.e. to his face; *directions* instruction 71 *expedition* readiness

tain his argument as well as any military man in the orld in the disciplines of the pristine wars of the Romans.

JAMY I say gud day, Captain Fluellen.

FLUELLEN God-den to your worship, good Captain James.

GOWER How now, Captain Macmorris? Have you quit the mines? Have the pioners given o'er?

MACMORRIS By Chrish, law, tish ill done! The work ish give over, the trompet sound the retreat. By my hand I swear, and my father's soul, the work ish ill done! It ish give over. I would have blowed up the town, so Chrish save me, law, in an hour. O, tish ill done! tish ill done! By my hand, tish ill done!

FLUELLEN Captain Macmorris, I beseech you now, will you voutsafe me, look you, a few disputations with you, as partly touching or concerning the disciplines of the war, the Roman wars? In the way of argument, look you, and friendly communication; partly to satisfy my opinion, and partly for the satisfaction, look you, of my mind, as touching the direction of the military discipline, that is the point.

JAMY It sall be vary gud, gud feith, gud captens bath, and I sall quit you with gud leve, as I may pick occasion. That sall I, mary.

MACMORRIS It is no time to discourse, so Chrish save me! The day is hot, and the weather, and the wars, and the king, and the dukes. It is no time to discourse. The town is beseeched, and the trompet call us to the breach, and we talk, and, be Chrish, do nothing. 'Tis shame for us all. So God sa' me, 'tis shame to stand still, it is shame, by my hand! and there is throats to be cut, and works to be done, and there ish nothing done, so Chrish sa' me, law!

JAMY By the mess, ere theise eyes of mine take themselves to slomber, ay'll de gud service, or ay'll lig i' th' grund

79 *pioners* sappers 90 *communication* consultation 95 *quit* answer 105 *mess* i.e. Mass

for it! ay, or go to death! And ay'll pay't as valorously as I may, that sall I suerly do, that is the breff and the long.
109 Mary, I wad full fain heard some question 'tween you tway.

FLUELLEN Captain Macmorris, I think, look you, under your correction, there is not many of your nation –

113 MACMORRIS Of my nation? What ish my nation? Ish a villain and a bastard, and a knave, and a rascal! What ish my nation? Who talks of my nation?

FLUELLEN Look you, if you take the matter otherwise than is meant, Captain Macmorris, peradventure I shall think you do not use me with that affability as in discretion you ought to use me, look you, being as good a man as yourself, poth in the disciplines of war, and in the derivation of my pirth, and in other particularities.

MACMORRIS I do not know you so good a man as myself. So Chrish save me, I will cut off your head!

124 GOWER Gentlemen both, you will mistake each other.

125 JAMY A', that's a foul fault!

A parley [sounded].

GOWER The town sounds a parley.

FLUELLEN Captain Macmorris, when there is more petter opportunity to be required, look you, I will be so pold as to tell you I know the disciplines of war; and there is an end. *Exit [with others].*

*

III, iii *Enter the King [Henry] and all his Train before the gates.*

KING

How yet resolves the governor of the town?
2 This is the latest parle we will admit:
Therefore to our best mercy give yourselves,

109 *question* discussion **113** *What ish* i.e. what about; *Ish* i.e. someone, not exclusively Fluellen, is (Macmorris' sensitivity about his nationality makes him discharge at a general target the insulting epithets which follow) **124** *will mistake* persist in misjudging **125** *A'* (equivalent to 'Ach')
III, iii Before the walls of Harfleur at the gates **2** *parle* parley

Or, like to men proud of destruction, 4
Defy us to our worst; for, as I am a soldier,
A name that in my thoughts becomes me best,
If I begin the batt'ry once again,
I will not leave the half-achievèd Harfleur
Till in her ashes she lie burièd.
The gates of mercy shall be all shut up,
And the fleshed soldier, rough and hard of heart, 11
In liberty of bloody hand shall range
With conscience wide as hell, mowing like grass 13
Your fresh fair virgins and your flow'ring infants.
What is it then to me if impious war,
Arrayed in flames to the prince of fiends,
Do with his smirched complexion all fell feats 17
Enlinked to waste and desolation?
What is't to me, when you yourselves are cause,
If your pure maidens fall into the hand
Of hot and forcing violation?
What rein can hold licentious wickedness
When down the hill he holds his fierce career? 23
We may as bootless spend our vain command 24
Upon th' engagèd soldiers in their spoil
As send precepts to the leviathan 26
To come ashore. Therefore, you men of Harfleur,
Take pity of your town and of your people
Whiles yet my soldiers are in my command,
Whiles yet the cool and temperate wind of grace 30
O'erblows the filthy and contagious clouds 31
Of heady murder, spoil, and villainy. 32
If not – why, in a moment look to see
The blind and bloody soldier with foul hand
Defile the locks of your shrill-shrieking daughters;
Your fathers taken by the silver beards,

4 *proud of* who glory in 11 *fleshed* hardened with killing 13 *wide* permissive 17 *smirched* sooty 23 *holds . . . career* maintains his fierce gallop 24 *bootless* uselessly 26 *precepts* written summons 30 *grace* mercy 31 *O'erblows* outblows 32 *heady* headstrong

And their most reverend heads dashed to the walls;
Your naked infants spitted upon pikes,
Whiles the mad mothers with their howls confused
Do break the clouds, as did the wives of Jewry
41 At Herod's bloody-hunting slaughtermen.
What say you? Will you yield, and this avoid?
43 Or, guilty in defense, be thus destroyed?

Enter Governor [on the wall].

GOVERNOR

Our expectation hath this day an end.
The Dauphin, whom of succors we entreated,
46 Returns us that his powers are not yet ready
To raise so great a siege. Therefore, great king,
We yield our town and lives to thy soft mercy.
Enter our gates, dispose of us and ours,
For we no longer are defensible.

KING

Open your gates. Come, uncle Exeter,
Go you and enter Harfleur; there remain
And fortify it strongly 'gainst the French.
Use mercy to them all. For us, dear uncle,
The winter coming on, and sickness growing
Upon our soldiers, we will retire to Calais.
To-night in Harfleur will we be your guest;
58 To-morrow for the march are we addrest.

Flourish, and enter the town.

*

III, iv *Enter Katherine and [Alice,] an old Gentlewoman.*

KATHERINE Alice, tu as esté en Angleterre, et tu bien parles le langage.

41 *Herod's . . . slaughtermen* (cf. Matthew ii, 16–18) 43 *in defense* i.e. of reckless defense 46 *Returns us* replies 58 *addrest* prepared
III, iv Within the palace of the French King KATH. Alice, you have been in England, and you speak the language well.

ALICE Un peu, madame.

KATHERINE Je te prie m'enseigner; il faut que j'apprends à parler. Comment appelez-vous le main en Anglois?

ALICE Le main? Il est appelé de hand.

KATHERINE De hand. Et les doigts?

ALICE Les doigts? Ma foi, j'oublie les doigts; mais je me souviendrai. Les doigts? Je pense qu'ils'ont appelé de fingres; oui, de fingres.

KATHERINE Le main, de hand; les doigts, de fingres. Je pense que je suis le bon escolier; j'ai gagné deux mots d'Anglois vistement. Comment appelez-vous les ongles?

ALICE Les ongles, les appelons de nailès.

KATHERINE De nailès. Escoute; dites-moi si je parle bien: de hand, de fingres, et de nailès.

ALICE C'est bien dict, madame; il est fort bon Anglois.

KATHERINE Dites-moi l'Anglois pour le bras.

ALICE De arm, madame.

KATHERINE Et le coude.

ALICE D' elbow.

KATHERINE D' elbow. Je me'en fais le répétition de tous les mots que vous m'avez apprins dès à présent.

ALICE Il est trop difficile, madame, comme je pense.

KATHERINE Excuse moi, Alice; escoute: d' hand, de fingre, de nailès, d' arma, de bilbow.

ALICE D' elbow, madame.

AL. A little, my lady. KATH. I beg you teach me; I must learn to speak it. What do you call *le main* in English? AL. *Le main*? It is called *de hand*. KATH. *De hand*. And *les doigts*? AL. *Les doigts*? My faith, I forget *les doigts;* but I will remember. *Les doigts*? I think they are called *de fingres;* yes, *de fingres*. KATH. *Le main, de hand; les doigts, de fingres*. I think I am a good scholar; I have learned two words of English quickly. What do you call *les ongles*? AL. *Les ongles* we call *de nailès*. KATH. *De nailès*. Listen; tell me if I speak well: *de hand, de fingres*, and *de nailès*. AL. Well spoken, my lady; it is very good English. KATH. Tell me the English for *le bras*. AL. *De arm*, my lady. KATH. And *le coude*. AL. *D'elbow*. KATH. *D'elbow*. I am going to repeat all the words you have taught me so far. AL. It is too hard, my lady, so I think. KATH. Excuse me, Alice; listen: *d'hand, de fingre, de nailès, d'arma, de bilbow*. AL. *D'elbow*, my lady.

KATHERINE O Seigneur Dieu, je m'en oublie d' elbow! Comment appelez-vous le col?

ALICE De nick, madame.

KATHERINE De nick. Et le menton?

ALICE De chin.

KATHERINE De sin. Le col, de nick; le menton, de sin.

ALICE Oui. Sauf vostre honneur, en vérité, vous prononcez les mots aussi droict que les natifs d'Angleterre.

KATHERINE Je ne doute point d'apprendre, par la grace de Dieu, et en peu de temps.

ALICE N'avez-vous pas déjà oublié ce que je vous ai enseigné?

KATHERINE Non, je réciterai à vous promptement: d' hand, de fingre, de mailès –

ALICE De nailès, madame.

KATHERINE De nailès, de arm, de ilbow –

ALICE Sauf vostre honneur, d' elbow.

KATHERINE Ainsi dis-je; d' elbow, de nick, et de sin. Comment appelez-vous le pied et la robe?

ALICE De foot, madame; et de count.

KATHERINE De foot et de count! O Seigneur Dieu! ils'ont les mots de son mauvais, corruptible, gros, et impudique, et non pour les dames d'honneur d'user: je ne voudrais prononcer ces mots devant les seigneurs de France pour tout le monde. Foh! de foot et de count!

KATH. O Lord God, I can't remember *d'elbow*. What do you call *le col*? AL. *De nick*, my lady. KATH. *De nick*. And *le menton*? AL. *De chin*. KATH. *De sin. Le col, de nick; le menton, de sin*. AL. Yes. Save your honor, indeed you pronounce the words as well as the native English. KATH. I trust to learn, by the grace of God, and in short time. AL. You have not already forgotten what I have taught you? KATH. No, I shall recite for you promptly: *d'hand, de fingre, de mailès* – AL. *De nailès*, my lady. KATH. *De nailès, de arm, de ilbow* – AL. Save your honor, *d'elbow*. KATH. So I said – *d'elbow, de nick, and de sin*. What do you call *le pied* and *la robe*? AL. *De foot*, my lady; and *de count* [i.e. gown]. KATH. *De foot* [which she mistakes for indecent '*foutre*'] and *de count*! O Lord God! they are bad words, wicked, coarse, and immodest, and not for ladies of honor to use: I would not speak those words before the gentlemen of France for all the world. Foh! *de foot* and *de count*!

Néantmoins, je réciterai une autre fois ma leçon ensemble: d' hand, de fingre, de nailès, d' arm, d' elbow, de nick, de sin, de foot, de count.

ALICE Excellent, madame!

KATHERINE C'est assez pour une fois: allons-nous à diner. *Exit [with Alice].*

*

III, v

Enter the King of France, the Dauphin [, Britaine], the Constable of France, and others.

KING
'Tis certain he hath passed the river Somme.

CONSTABLE
And if he be not fought withal, my lord.
Let us not live in France; let us quit all
And give our vineyards to a barbarous people.

DAUPHIN
O Dieu vivant! Shall a few sprays of us,
The emptying of our fathers' luxury,
Our scions, put in wild and savage stock,
Spurt up so suddenly into the clouds
And overlook their grafters?

BRITAINE
Normans, but bastard Normans, Norman bastards!
Mort de ma vie! if they march along
Unfought withal, but I will sell my dukedom
To buy a slobb'ry and a dirty farm
In that nook-shotten isle of Albion.

CONSTABLE
Dieu de batailles! where have they this mettle?

Nevertheless, I will recite once more my entire lesson: *d'hand, de fingre, de nailès, d'arm, d'elbow, de nick, de sin, de foot, de count*. AL. Excellent, my lady! KATH. That's enough for one time; let's go to dinner.

III, v The French King's quarters at Rouen 1 *passed . . . Somme* (in the withdrawal to Calais) 5 *sprays* offshoots 6 *fathers' luxury* i.e. forefathers' lust 7 *scions* grafts 11 *Mort . . . vie* death of my life 13 *slobb'ry* slovenly 14 *nook-shotten* full of nooks, i.e. with a ragged coastline 15 *batailles* battles

Is not their climate foggy, raw, and dull,
On whom, as in despite, the sun looks pale,
18 Killing their fruit with frowns? Can sodden water,
19 A drench for sur-reined jades, their barley broth,
20 Decoct their cold blood to such valiant heat?
And shall our quick blood, spirited with wine,
Seem frosty? O, for honor of our land,
23 Let us not hang like roping icicles
Upon our houses' thatch, whiles a more frosty people
Sweat drops of gallant youth in our rich fields –
26 'Poor' we call them in their native lords!

DAUPHIN
By faith and honor,
Our madams mock at us and plainly say
Our mettle is bred out, and they will give
Their bodies to the lust of English youth
To new-store France with bastard warriors.

BRITAINE
They bid us to the English dancing schools
33 And teach lavoltas high, and swift corantos,
34 Saying our grace is only in our heels
And that we are most lofty runaways.

KING
Where is Montjoy the herald? Speed him hence;
Let him greet England with our sharp defiance.
Up, princes! and with spirit of honor edged
More sharper than your swords, hie to the field.
Charles Delabreth, High Constable of France,
You Dukes of Orleans, Bourbon, and of Berri,
Alençon, Brabant, Bar, and Burgundy;
Jacques Chatillon, Rambures, Vaudemont,
Beaumont, Grandpré, Roussi, and Faulconbridge,

18 *sodden* boiled **19** *drench . . . jades* draught for exhausted horses; *barley broth* ale (sometimes used as a drench) **20** *Decoct* infuse **23** *roping* spun out by dripping **26** *'Poor' . . . lords* i.e. but not rich in their possessors **33** *And* i.e. to; *lavoltas* dance characterized by leaps; *corantos* dance characterized by running steps **34** *in our heels* (1) as dancers, (2) as those who 'take to their heels'

Foix, Lestrale, Bouciqualt, and Charolois,
High dukes, great princes, barons, lords, and knights,
For your great seats now quit you of great shames.
Bar Harry England, that sweeps through our land
With pennons painted in the blood of Harfleur.
Rush on his host as doth the melted snow
Upon the valleys whose low vassal seat
The Alps doth spit and void his rheum upon.
Go down upon him – you have power enough –
And in a captive chariot into Rouen
Bring him our prisoner.

CONSTABLE This becomes the great.
Sorry am I his numbers are so few,
His soldiers sick and famished in their march;
For I am sure, when he shall see our army,
He'll drop his heart into the sink of fear
And, for achievement, offer us his ransom.

KING
Therefore, Lord Constable, haste on Montjoy,
And let him say to England that we send
To know what willing ransom he will give.
Prince Dauphin, you shall stay with us in Rouen.

DAUPHIN
Not so, I do beseech your majesty.

KING
Be patient, for you shall remain with us.
Now forth, Lord Constable and princes all,
And quickly bring us word of England's fall. *Exeunt.*

*

III, vi

Enter Captains, English and Welsh – Gower and Fluellen.

GOWER How now, Captain Fluellen? Come you from the bridge?

47 *quit* acquit 59 *sink* pit 60 *for achievement* i.e. instead of conquering
III, vi The English camp in Picardy

FLUELLEN I assure you there is very excellent services committed at the pridge.

GOWER Is the Duke of Exeter safe?

FLUELLEN The Duke of Exeter is as magnanimous as Agamemnon, and a man that I love and honor with my soul, and my heart, and my duty, and my live, and my living, and my uttermost power. He is not – God be praised and plessed! – any hurt in the orld, but keeps the pridge most valiantly, with excellent discipline. There is an aunchient lieutenant there at the pridge, I think in my very conscience he is as valiant a man as Mark Anthony, and he is a man of no estimation in the orld, but I did see him do as gallant service.

GOWER What do you call him?

FLUELLEN He is called Aunchient Pistol.

GOWER I know him not.

Enter Pistol.

FLUELLEN Here is the man.

PISTOL

Captain, I thee beseech to do me favors.
The Duke of Exeter doth love thee well.

FLUELLEN Ay, I praise God; and I have merited some love at his hands.

PISTOL

Bardolph, a soldier firm and sound of heart,
And of buxom valor, hath by cruel fate,
And giddy Fortune's furious fickle wheel –
That goddess blind,
That stands upon the rolling restless stone –

FLUELLEN By your patience, Aunchient Pistol. Fortune is painted plind, with a muffler afore her eyes, to signify to you that Fortune is plind; and she is painted also with a wheel, to signify to you, which is the moral of it, that she is turning and inconstant, and mutability, and

8 *live* i.e. life 12 *aunchient lieutenant* (Pistol is elsewhere ranked simply as 'ancient,' i.e. ensign) 14 *estimation* fame 15 *gallant service* i.e. with words (cf. ll. 62–63)

variation; and her foot, look you, is fixed upon a spherical stone, which rolls, and rolls, and rolls. In good truth, the poet makes a most excellent description of it. Fortune is an excellent moral. 37

PISTOL
Fortune is Bardolph's foe, and frowns on him; 38
For he hath stol'n a pax, and hangèd must 'a be – 39
A damnèd death!
Let gallows gape for dog; let man go free,
And let not hemp his windpipe suffocate.
But Exeter hath given the doom of death 43
For pax of little price.
Therefore, go speak – the duke will hear thy voice;
And let not Bardolph's vital thread be cut
With edge of penny cord and vile reproach.
Speak, captain, for his life, and I will thee requite.

FLUELLEN Aunchient Pistol, I do partly understand your meaning.

PISTOL
Why then, rejoice therefore!

FLUELLEN Certainly, Aunchient, it is not a thing to rejoice at; for if, look you, he were my prother, I would desire the duke to use his good pleasure and put him to execution; for discipline ought to be used.

PISTOL
Die and be damned! and figo for thy friendship! 56

FLUELLEN It is well.

PISTOL
The fig of Spain! *Exit.*

FLUELLEN Very good.

GOWER Why, this is an arrant counterfeit rascal! I remember him now – a bawd, a cutpurse.

37 *moral* i.e. emblem of instruction (the goddess Fortune figured prominently in literary and pictorial admonitions about the mutability of life) 38 *foe . . . frowns* (reminiscent of popular ballad, 'Fortune, my foe, why dost thou frown on me?') 39 *pax* metal disk engraved with crucifix, kissed during celebration of Mass 43 *doom* sentence 56 *figo* i.e. Spanish for fig (epithet and gesture of contempt)

FLUELLEN I'll assure you, 'a uttered as prave words at the pridge as you shall see in a summer's day. But it is very well. What he has spoke to me, that is well, I warrant you, when time is serve.

GOWER Why, 'tis a gull, a fool, a rogue, that now and then
goes to the wars to grace himself, at his return into London, under the form of a soldier. And such fellows are
69 perfit in the great commanders' names, and they will
learn you by rote where services were done: at such
71 and such a sconce, at such a breach, at such a convoy; who
came off bravely, who was shot, who disgraced, what
terms the enemy stood on; and this they con perfitly in
the phrase of war, which they trick up with new-tuned
75 oaths; and what a beard of the general's cut and a horrid
suit of the camp will do among foaming bottles and ale-
washed wits is wonderful to be thought on. But you
78 must learn to know such slanders of the age, or else you
may be marvellously mistook.

FLUELLEN I tell you what, Captain Gower, I do perceive
he is not the man that he would gladly make show to the
82 orld he is. If I find a hole in his coat, I will tell him my
mind. *[Drum within.]* Hark you, the king is coming, and
I must speak with him from the pridge.

Drum and Colors. Enter the King and his poor Soldiers [and Gloucester].

God pless your majesty!

KING
How now, Fluellen? Cam'st thou from the bridge?

FLUELLEN Ay, so please your majesty. The Duke of
Exeter has very gallantly maintained the pridge; the
French is gone off, look you, and there is gallant and
90 most prave passages. Marry, th' athversary was have
possession of the pridge, but he is enforced to retire,

69 *perfit* word-perfect 71 *sconce* earthwork; *convoy* transport of troops 75–76 *horrid suit* fierce attire 78 *slanders* disgraces 82 *a hole . . . coat* i.e. a means of exposing him 90 *passages* (of arms)

and the Duke of Exeter is master of the pridge. I can tell your majesty, the duke is a prave man.

KING What men have you lost, Fluellen?

FLUELLEN The perdition of th' athversary hath been very great, reasonable great. Marry, for my part, I think the duke hath lost never a man but one that is like to be executed for robbing a church – one Pardolph, if your majesty know the man. His face is all bubukles and whelks, and knobs, and flames o' fire, and his lips plows at his nose, and it is like a coal of fire, sometimes plue and sometimes red; but his nose is executed, and his fire 's out.

KING We would have all such offenders so cut off. And we give express charge that in our marches through the country there be nothing compelled from the villages, nothing taken but paid for; none of the French upbraided or abused in disdainful language; for when lenity and cruelty play for a kingdom, the gentler gamester is the soonest winner.

Tucket. Enter Montjoy.

MONTJOY You know me by my habit.

KING Well then, I know thee. What shall I know of thee?

MONTJOY My master's mind.

KING Unfold it.

MONTJOY Thus says my king: Say thou to Harry of England: Though we seemed dead, we did but sleep. Advantage is a better soldier than rashness. Tell him we could have rebuked him at Harfleur, but that we thought not good to bruise an injury till it were full ripe. Now we speak upon our cue, and our voice is imperial. England shall repent his folly, see his weakness, and admire our sufferance. Bid him therefore consider of his ransom,

95 *perdition* loss, casualties 99 *bubukles and whelks* carbuncles and pimples 109 s.d. *Tucket* trumpet call 110 *habit* attire 115 *Advantage* circumspection 118 *bruise* squeeze (as in treating a boil) 120–21 *admire . . . sufferance* wonder at our patience

which must proportion the losses we have borne, the sub-
123 jects we have lost, the disgrace we have digested; which in weight to re-answer, his pettiness would bow under. For our losses, his exchequer is too poor; for th' effusion of our blood, the muster of his kingdom too faint a number; and for our disgrace, his own person kneeling at our feet but a weak and worthless satisfaction. To this add defiance; and tell him for conclusion he hath betrayed his followers, whose condemnation is pronounced. So far my king and master; so much my office.

KING
132 What is thy name? I know thy quality.

MONTJOY Montjoy.

KING
Thou dost thy office fairly. Turn thee back,
And tell thy king I do not seek him now,
But could be willing to march on to Calais
137 Without impeachment: for, to say the sooth,
Though 'tis no wisdom to confess so much
139 Unto an enemy of craft and vantage,
My people are with sickness much enfeebled,
My numbers lessened, and those few I have
Almost no better than so many French,
Who when they were in health, I tell thee, herald,
I thought upon one pair of English legs
Did march three Frenchmen. Yet forgive me, God,
That I do brag thus! This your air of France
147 Hath blown that vice in me. I must repent.
Go therefore tell thy master here I am;
My ransom is this frail and worthless trunk;
My army but a weak and sickly guard;
Yet, God before, tell him we will come on,
Though France himself and such another neighbor
Stand in our way. There's for thy labor, Montjoy.

123–24 *which . . . under* i.e. to compensate for which his means are too small
132 *quality* rank 137 *impeachment* challenge 139 *vantage* superiority in numbers 147 *blown* brought to bloom

[Gives a purse.]
Go bid thy master well advise himself: 154
If we may pass, we will; if we be hind'red,
We shall your tawny ground with your red blood
Discolor; and so, Montjoy, fare you well.
The sum of all our answer is but this:
We would not seek a battle as we are,
Nor, as we are, we say we will not shun it.
So tell your master.

MONTJOY
I shall deliver so. Thanks to your highness. *[Exit.]*

GLOUCESTER
I hope they will not come upon us now.

KING
We are in God's hand, brother, not in theirs.
March to the bridge. It now draws toward night.
Beyond the river we'll encamp ourselves,
And on to-morrow bid them march away. *Exeunt.*

*

Enter the Constable of France, the Lord Rambures, Orleans, Dauphin, with others. III, vii

CONSTABLE Tut! I have the best armor of the world. Would it were day!

ORLEANS You have an excellent armor; but let my horse have his due.

CONSTABLE It is the best horse of Europe.

ORLEANS Will it never be morning?

DAUPHIN My Lord of Orleans, and my Lord High Constable, you talk of horse and armor?

ORLEANS You are well provided of both as any prince in the world.

DAUPHIN What a long night is this! I will not change my horse with any that treads but on four pasterns. Ça, ha!

154 *advise himself* consider
III, vii The French camp near Agincourt

he bounds from the earth, as if his entrails were hairs; le cheval volant, the Pegasus, chez les narines de feu! When I bestride him, I soar, I am a hawk. He trots the air. The earth sings when he touches it. The basest horn of his hoof is more musical than the pipe of Hermes.

ORLEANS He's of the color of the nutmeg.

DAUPHIN And of the heat of the ginger. It is a beast for Perseus: he is pure air and fire; and the dull elements of earth and water never appear in him, but only in patient stillness while his rider mounts him. He is indeed a horse, and all other jades you may call beasts.

CONSTABLE Indeed, my lord, it is a most absolute and excellent horse.

DAUPHIN It is the prince of palfreys. His neigh is like the bidding of a monarch, and his countenance enforces homage.

ORLEANS No more, cousin.

DAUPHIN Nay, the man hath no wit that cannot, from the rising of the lark to the lodging of the lamb, vary deserved praise on my palfrey. It is a theme as fluent as the sea. Turn the sands into eloquent tongues, and my horse is argument for them all. 'Tis a subject for a sovereign to reason on, and for a sovereign's sovereign to ride on; and for the world, familiar to us and unknown, to lay apart their particular functions and wonder at him. I once writ a sonnet in his praise and began thus, 'Wonder of nature!'

ORLEANS I have heard a sonnet begin so to one's mistress.

DAUPHIN Then did they imitate that which I composed to my courser, for my horse is my mistress.

13 *hairs* (like the stuffing of a tennis ball) 14 *le cheval . . . feu* the flying horse, Pegasus, with nostrils of fire 16 *basest horn* i.e. hoofbeat (with pun on the musical instrument) 17 *pipe* (the musical instrument with which Hermes, i.e. Mercury, lulled to sleep the monster Argus) 20 *Perseus* (in Ovid, the rider of Pegasus while rescuing Andromeda from a dragon) 24 *absolute* perfect 26 *palfreys* saddle-horses 31 *lodging* i.e. going to bed 35 *reason on* discourse upon 36–37 *to lay . . . functions* i.e. to combine

ORLEANS Your mistress bears well.

DAUPHIN Me well, which is the prescript praise and perfection of a good and particular mistress.

CONSTABLE Nay, for methought yesterday your mistress shrewdly shook your back.

DAUPHIN So perhaps did yours.

CONSTABLE Mine was not bridled.

DAUPHIN O, then belike she was old and gentle, and you rode like a kern of Ireland, your French hose off, and in your strait strossers.

CONSTABLE You have good judgment in horsemanship.

DAUPHIN Be warned by me then. They that ride so, and ride not warily, fall into foul bogs. I had rather have my horse to my mistress.

CONSTABLE I had as lief have my mistress a jade.

DAUPHIN I tell thee, Constable, my mistress wears his own hair.

CONSTABLE I could make as true a boast as that, if I had a sow to my mistress.

DAUPHIN 'Le chien est retourné à son propre vomissement, et la truie lavée au bourbier.' Thou mak'st use of anything.

CONSTABLE Yet do I not use my horse for my mistress, or any such proverb so little kin to the purpose.

RAMBURES My Lord Constable, the armor that I saw in your tent to-night – are those stars or suns upon it?

CONSTABLE Stars, my lord.

DAUPHIN Some of them will fall to-morrow, I hope.

CONSTABLE And yet my sky shall not want.

DAUPHIN That may be, for you bear a many superfluously, and 'twere more honor some were away.

44 *prescript* appropriate 47 *shrewdly* grievously 51 *kern* Irish bush-fighter; *French hose* breeches 52 *strait strossers* tight trousers, i.e. bare-legged 56 *to* as 62–63 *Le chien . . . bourbier* the dog is returned to his own vomit and the washed sow to the mire (2 Peter ii, 22) 71 *want* be lacking (in stars, i.e. honors)

CONSTABLE Ev'n as your horse bears your praises, who would trot as well, were some of your brags dismounted.

DAUPHIN Would I were able to load him with his desert! Will it never be day? I will trot to-morrow a mile, and my way shall be paved with English faces.

79 CONSTABLE I will not say so, for fear I should be faced out of my way: but I would it were morning, for I would fain be about the ears of the English.

82 RAMBURES Who will go to hazard with me for twenty prisoners?

CONSTABLE You must first go yourself to hazard ere you have them.

DAUPHIN 'Tis midnight; I'll go arm myself. *Exit.*

ORLEANS The Dauphin longs for morning.

RAMBURES He longs to eat the English.

CONSTABLE I think he will eat all he kills.

ORLEANS By the white hand of my lady, he's a gallant prince.

CONSTABLE Swear by her foot, that she may tread out the oath.

ORLEANS He is simply the most active gentleman of France.

95 CONSTABLE Doing is activity, and he will still be doing.

ORLEANS He never did harm, that I heard of.

CONSTABLE Nor will do none to-morrow. He will keep that good name still.

ORLEANS I know him to be valiant.

CONSTABLE I was told that by one that knows him better than you.

ORLEANS What's he?

CONSTABLE Marry, he told me so himself, and he said he cared not who knew it.

ORLEANS He needs not; it is no hidden virtue in him.

106 CONSTABLE By my faith, sir, but it is! Never anybody

79 *faced* braved **82** *go to hazard* play at dice **95** *Doing* i.e. acting, pretending **106–07** *Never . . . lackey* i.e. he is valiant only with his lackey

saw it but his lackey. 'Tis a hooded valor; and when it appears, it will bate.

ORLEANS Ill will never said well.

CONSTABLE I will cap that proverb with 'There is flattery in friendship.'

ORLEANS And I will take up that with 'Give the devil his due.'

CONSTABLE Well placed! There stands your friend for the devil. Have at the very eye of that proverb with 'A pox of the devil!'

ORLEANS You are the better at proverbs, by how much 'a fool's bolt is soon shot.'

CONSTABLE You have shot over.

ORLEANS 'Tis not the first time you were overshot.

Enter a Messenger.

MESSENGER My Lord High Constable, the English lie within fifteen hundred paces of your tents.

CONSTABLE Who hath measured the ground?

MESSENGER The Lord Grandpré.

CONSTABLE A valiant and most expert gentleman. Would it were day! Alas, poor Harry of England! He longs not for the dawning, as we do.

ORLEANS What a wretched and peevish fellow is this king of England, to mope with his fat-brained followers so far out of his knowledge!

CONSTABLE If the English had any apprehension, they would run away.

ORLEANS That they lack; for if their heads had any intellectual armor, they could never wear such heavy head-pieces.

107 *hooded* with head covered, i.e. like a quiescent hawk 108 *bate* flutter, i.e. like a hawk when unhooded (with pun on 'bate' in sense of 'diminish') 114 *Well placed* well played, i.e. appropriate 115 *Have . . . eye* i.e. right on the mark (another sporting term evoked by this contest in proverb-capping) 119 *shot over* i.e. over the mark 120 *overshot* i.e. defeated 128 *peevish* silly 129 *mope* grope about 130 *out . . . knowledge* i.e. over his head 131 *apprehension* understanding

RAMBURES That island of England breeds very valiant creatures. Their mastiffs are of unmatchable courage.

138 ORLEANS Foolish curs, that run winking into the mouth of a Russian bear and have their heads crushed like rotten apples! You may as well say that's a valiant flea that dare eat his breakfast on the lip of a lion.

142 CONSTABLE Just, just! and the men do sympathize with the mastiffs in robustious and rough coming on, leaving their wits with their wives; and then give them great meals of beef and iron and steel, they will eat like wolves and fight like devils.

147 ORLEANS Ay, but these English are shrewdly out of beef.

CONSTABLE Then shall we find to-morrow they have only stomachs to eat and none to fight. Now is it time to arm. Come, shall we about it?

ORLEANS

It is now two o'clock; but let me see – by ten
We shall have each a hundred Englishmen. *Exeunt.*

*

IV, Cho. *Chorus.*

1 Now entertain conjecture of a time
2 When creeping murmur and the poring dark
Fills the wide vessel of the universe.
From camp to camp, through the foul womb of night,
5 The hum of either army stilly sounds,
6 That the fixed sentinels almost receive
The secret whispers of each other's watch.
8 Fire answers fire, and through their paly flames
9 Each battle sees the other's umbered face.

138 *winking* with eyes shut 142 *sympathize* i.e. have fellow-feeling 147 *shrewdly* grievously

IV, Cho. 1 *entertain conjecture of* imagine 2 *poring* peering 5 *stilly* quietly 6 *That* so that 8 *paly* pale (with play on heraldic meaning of alternately tinctured vertical lines?) 9 *battle* army; *umbered* shadowed (with play on 'umbred,' i.e. visored?, or on heraldic 'umbrated,' i.e. outlined, here silhouetted?)

Steed threatens steed, in high and boastful neighs
Piercing the night's dull ear; and from the tents
The armorers accomplishing the knights, 12
With busy hammers closing rivets up,
Give dreadful note of preparation.
The country cocks do crow, the clocks do toll
And the third hour of drowsy morning name.
Proud of their numbers and secure in soul, 17
The confident and over-lusty French 18
Do the low-rated English play at dice; 19
And chide the cripple tardy-gaited night
Who like a foul and ugly witch doth limp
So tediously away. The poor condemnèd English,
Like sacrifices, by their watchful fires
Sit patiently and inly ruminate
The morning's danger; and their gesture sad,
Investing lank-lean cheeks and war-worn coats,
Presenteth them unto the gazing moon
So many horrid ghosts. O, now, who will behold 28
The royal captain of this ruined band
Walking from watch to watch, from tent to tent,
Let him cry, 'Praise and glory on his head!'
For forth he goes and visits all his host,
Bids them good morrow with a modest smile
And calls them brothers, friends, and countrymen.
Upon his royal face there is no note
How dread an army hath enrounded him; 36
Nor doth he dedicate one jot of color 37
Unto the weary and all-watchèd night,
But freshly looks, and overbears attaint 39
With cheerful semblance and sweet majesty;
That every wretch, pining and pale before,
Beholding him, plucks comfort from his looks.
A largess universal, like the sun.

12 *accomplishing* equipping 17 *secure in soul* confident in spirit 18 *over-lusty* over-lively 19 *play* i.e. play for 28 *horrid* fearful 36 *enrounded* surrounded 37 *dedicate* yield up 39 *overbears attaint* masters fatigue

His liberal eye doth give to every one,
Thawing cold fear, that mean and gentle all
46 Behold, as may unworthiness define,
47 A little touch of Harry in the night.
And so our scene must to the battle fly;
Where (O for pity!) we shall much disgrace
With four or five most vile and ragged foils,
Right ill-disposed in brawl ridiculous,
The name of Agincourt. Yet sit and see,
53 Minding true things by what their mock'ries be. *Exit.*

IV, i *Enter the King, Bedford, and Gloucester.*

KING
Gloucester, 'tis true that we are in great danger;
The greater therefore should our courage be.
Good morrow, brother Bedford. God Almighty!
There is some soul of goodness in things evil,
Would men observingly distill it out;
For our bad neighbor makes us early stirrers,
7 Which is both healthful, and good husbandry.
Besides, they are our outward consciences,
And preachers to us all, admonishing
10 That we should dress us fairly for our end.
Thus may we gather honey from the weed
And make a moral of the devil himself.
Enter Erpingham.
Good morrow, old Sir Thomas Erpingham.
A good soft pillow for that good white head
Were better than a churlish turf of France.

ERPINGHAM
Not so, my liege. This lodging likes me better,

46 *as . . . define* as it may be roughly expressed **47** *touch* i.e. essence **53** *Minding* bearing in mind; *mock'ries* absurd imitations
IV, i The English camp near Agincourt **7** *husbandry* good management
10 *dress us* prepare ourselves

Since I may say, 'Now lie I like a king.'

KING

'Tis good for men to love their present pains
Upon example: so the spirit is eased; 19
And when the mind is quick'ned, out of doubt 20
The organs, though defunct and dead before,
Break up their drowsy grave and newly move 22
With casted slough and fresh legerity. 23
Lend me thy cloak, Sir Thomas. Brothers both,
Commend me to the princes in our camp;
Do my good morrow to them, and anon
Desire them all to my pavilion.

GLOUCESTER

We shall, my liege.

ERPINGHAM

Shall I attend your grace?

KING No, my good knight.
Go with my brothers to my lords of England.
I and my bosom must debate awhile, 31
And then I would no other company.

ERPINGHAM

The Lord in heaven bless thee, noble Harry!

Exeunt [all but the King].

KING

God-a-mercy, old heart! thou speak'st cheerfully.

Enter Pistol.

PISTOL Che vous la? 35

KING A friend.

PISTOL

Discuss unto me, art thou officer;
Or art thou base, common, and popular? 38

KING I am a gentleman of a company.

19 *Upon example* in exemplary fashion **20** *quick'ned* enlivened **22** *Break . . . grave* break out of their grave of lethargy **23** *casted slough* discarded old skin; *legerity* briskness **31** *bosom* i.e. inner self, soul **35** *Che vous la* (Pistol's version of '*Qui va là*,' i.e. who goes there) **38** *popular* plebeian

PISTOL
Trail'st thou the puissant pike?
KING Even so. What are you?
PISTOL
As good a gentleman as the emperor.
KING Then you are a better than the king.
PISTOL
The king 's a bawcock, and a heart of gold,
A lad of life, an imp of fame,
Of parents good, of fist most valiant.
I kiss his dirty shoe, and from heartstring
I love the lovely bully. What is thy name?
KING Harry le Roy.
PISTOL
Le Roy? A Cornish name. Art thou of Cornish crew?
KING No, I am a Welshman.
PISTOL
Know'st thou Fluellen?
KING Yes.
PISTOL
Tell him I'll knock his leek about his pate
Upon Saint Davy's day.
KING Do not you wear your dagger in your cap that day, lest he knock that about yours.
PISTOL
Art thou his friend?
KING And his kinsman too.
PISTOL
The figo for thee then!
KING I thank you. God be with you!
PISTOL
My name is Pistol called.

40 *Trail'st . . . pike* i.e. are you an infantryman 44 *bawcock* fine fellow (cf. III, ii, 22) 45 *imp* child 47 *heartstring* i.e. the very cords of my heart 51 *a Welshman* (technically true, like his reply 'Harry le Roy'; cf. IV, vii, 100) 55 *Saint Davy's day* March 1, the Welsh national holiday 60 *figo* (cf. III, vi, 56)

KING It sorts well with your fierceness.

Exit [Pistol]. Manet King [aside].

Enter Fluellen and Gower.

GOWER Captain Fluellen!

FLUELLEN So! in the name of Cheshu Christ, speak fewer. It is the greatest admiration in the universal orld, when the true and aunchient prerogatifes and laws of the wars is not kept. If you would take the pains but to examine the wars of Pompey the Great, you shall find, I warrant you, that there is no tiddle taddle nor pibble pabble in Pompey's camp. I warrant you, you shall find the ceremonies of the wars, and the cares of it, and the forms of it, and the sobriety of it, and the modesty of it, to be otherwise.

GOWER Why, the enemy is loud; you hear him all night.

FLUELLEN If the enemy is an ass and a fool and a prating coxcomb, is it meet, think you, that we should also, look you, be an ass and a fool and a prating coxcomb? In your own conscience now?

GOWER I will speak lower.

FLUELLEN I pray you and beseech you that you will.

Exit [with Gower].

KING

Though it appear a little out of fashion,
There is much care and valor in this Welshman.

Enter three Soldiers, John Bates, Alexander Court, and Michael Williams.

COURT Brother John Bates, is not that the morning which breaks yonder?

BATES I think it be; but we have no great cause to desire the approach of day.

WILLIAMS We see yonder the beginning of the day, but I think we shall never see the end of it. Who goes there?

KING A friend.

WILLIAMS Under what captain serve you?

63 *sorts* suits 66 *admiration* wonder 70–71 *pibble pabble* bibble babble, chatter 77 *In* on

KING Under Sir Thomas Erpingham.

WILLIAMS A good old commander and a most kind
93 gentleman. I pray you, what thinks he of our estate?

KING Even as men wracked upon a sand, that look to be
washed off the next tide.

BATES He hath not told his thought to the king?

KING No; nor it is not meet he should. For though I speak
it to you, I think the king is but a man, as I am. The violet
99 smells to him as it doth to me; the element shows to him
100 as it doth to me; all his senses have but human condi-
101 tions. His ceremonies laid by, in his nakedness he ap-
102 pears but a man; and though his affections are higher
103 mounted than ours, yet when they stoop, they stoop
with the like wing. Therefore, when he sees reason of
fears, as we do, his fears, out of doubt, be of the same
106 relish as ours are. Yet, in reason, no man should possess
him with any appearance of fear, lest he, by showing it,
should dishearten his army.

BATES He may show what outward courage he will; but I
believe, as cold a night as 'tis, he could wish himself in
Thames up to the neck; and so I would he were, and I
111 by him, at all adventures, so we were quit here.

KING By my troth, I will speak my conscience of the
king: I think he would not wish himself anywhere but
where he is.

BATES Then I would he were here alone. So should he be
sure to be ransomed, and a many poor men's lives saved.

KING I dare say you love him not so ill to wish him here
alone, howsoever you speak this to feel other men's
minds. Methinks I could not die anywhere so contented
as in the king's company, his cause being just and his
quarrel honorable

93 *estate* state 99 *element shows* sky appears 100 *conditions* i.e. limitations 101 *ceremonies* observances due royalty 102 *affections* emotions 103 *stoop* swoop downward (hawking term) 106 *relish* taste 106–07 *possess him with* induce in him 111 *at all adventures* by all means

WILLIAMS That's more than we know.

BATES Ay, or more than we should seek after, for we know enough if we know we are the king's subjects. If his cause be wrong, our obedience to the king wipes the crime of it out of us.

WILLIAMS But if the cause be not good, the king himself hath a heavy reckoning to make when all those legs and arms and heads, chopped off in a battle, shall join together at the latter day and cry all, 'We died at such a place,' some swearing, some crying for a surgeon, some upon their wives left poor behind them, some upon the debts they owe, some upon their children rawly left. I am afeard there are few die well that die in a battle; for how can they charitably dispose of anything when blood is their argument? Now, if these men do not die well, it will be a black matter for the king that led them to it; who to disobey were against all proportion of subjection.

KING So, if a son that is by his father sent about merchandise do sinfully miscarry upon the sea, the imputation of his wickedness, by your rule, should be imposed upon his father that sent him; or if a servant, under his master's command transporting a sum of money, be assailed by robbers and die in many irreconciled iniquities, you may call the business of the master the author of the servant's damnation. But this is not so. The king is not bound to answer the particular endings of his soldiers, the father of his son, nor the master of his servant; for they purpose not their death when they purpose their services. Besides, there is no king, be his cause never so spotless, if it come to the arbitrement of swords, can try it out with all unspotted soldiers. Some peradventure have on them the guilt of premeditated and contrived murder; some, of beguiling virgins with the broken seals of perjury; some, making the wars their bulwark, that have before

130 *latter* last 133 *rawly* unprepared 135 *charitably* in Christian love
138 *proportion of subjection* due obedience 144 *irreconciled* unabsolved

gored the gentle bosom of peace with pillage and rob-
157 bery. Now, if these men have defeated the law and out-
158 run native punishment, though they can outstrip men,
they have no wings to fly from God. War is his beadle,
war is his vengeance; so that here men are punished for
before-breach of the king's laws in now the king's quarrel. Where they feared the death, they have borne life
away; and where they would be safe, they perish. Then
164 if they die unprovided, no more is the king guilty of
their damnation than he was before guilty of those im-
pieties for the which they are now visited. Every subject's duty is the king's, but every subject's soul is his
own. Therefore should every soldier in the wars do as
169 every sick man in his bed – wash every mote out of his
170 conscience; and dying so, death is to him advantage; or
not dying, the time was blessedly lost wherein such
preparation was gained; and in him that escapes, it
were not sin to think that, making God so free an offer,
he let him outlive that day to see his greatness and to
teach others how they should prepare.

WILLIAMS 'Tis certain, every man that dies ill, the ill upon his own head – the king is not to answer it.

BATES I do not desire he should answer for me, and yet I determine to fight lustily for him.

KING I myself heard the king say he would not be ransomed.

WILLIAMS Ay, he said so, to make us fight cheerfully; but when our throats are cut, he may be ransomed, and we ne'er the wiser.

KING If I live to see it, I will never trust his word after.

WILLIAMS You pay him then! That's a perilous shot out
187 of an elder-gun that a poor and a private displeasure can
do against a monarch! You may as well go about to turn
the sun to ice with fanning in his face with a peacock's

157 *defeated* broken 158 *native* in their own country 164 *unprovided* unprepared 169 *mote* small impurity 170 *advantage* a gain (in that he dies prepared) 187 *elder-gun* pop-gun

feather. You'll never trust his word after! Come, 'tis a
foolish saying.

KING Your reproof is something too round. I should be 192
angry with you if the time were convenient.

WILLIAMS Let it be a quarrel between us if you live.

KING I embrace it.

WILLIAMS How shall I know thee again?

KING Give me any gage of thine, and I will wear it in my 197
bonnet. Then, if ever thou dar'st acknowledge it, I will
make it my quarrel.

WILLIAMS Here's my glove. Give me another of thine.

KING There.

WILLIAMS This will I also wear in my cap. If ever thou come to me and say, after to-morrow, 'This is my glove,' by this hand, I will take thee a box on the ear.

KING If ever I live to see it, I will challenge it.

WILLIAMS Thou dar'st as well be hanged.

KING Well, I will do it, though I take thee in the king's company.

WILLIAMS Keep thy word. Fare thee well.

BATES Be friends, you English fools, be friends! We have
French quarrels enow, if you could tell how to reckon. 211

KING Indeed the French may lay twenty French crowns to 212
one they will beat us, for they bear them on their shoul-
ders; but it is no English treason to cut French crowns, 214
and to-morrow the king himself will be a clipper.

Exit [Bates with other] Soldiers.

Upon the king! Let us our lives, our souls,
Our debts, our careful wives, 217
Our children, and our sins, lay on the king!
We must bear all. O hard condition,
Twin-born with greatness, subject to the breath
Of every fool, whose sense no more can feel

192 *round* unsparing 197 *gage* token of challenge 211 *enow* enough 212 *crowns* gold pieces (with play on 'heads' since the English are outnumbered) 214 *cut* i.e. clip edges of (a crime against the monarch's coinage classified as treason) 217 *careful* careworn

222 But his own wringing! What infinite heart's-ease
Must kings neglect that private men enjoy!
And what have kings that privates have not too,
225 Save ceremony, save general ceremony?
And what art thou, thou idol Ceremony?
What kind of god art thou, that suffer'st more
Of mortal griefs than do thy worshippers?
What are thy rents? What are thy comings-in?
O Ceremony, show me but thy worth!
231 What is thy soul of adoration?
Art thou aught else but place, degree, and form,
Creating awe and fear in other men?
Wherein thou art less happy being feared
Than they in fearing.
What drink'st thou oft, instead of homage sweet,
But poisoned flattery? O, be sick, great greatness,
And bid thy ceremony give thee cure!
Think'st thou the fiery fever will go out
With titles blown from adulation?
241 Will it give place to flexure and low bending?
Canst thou, when thou command'st the beggar's knee,
Command the health of it? No, thou proud dream,
That play'st so subtilly with a king's repose.
245 I am a king that find thee; and I know
246 'Tis not the balm, the sceptre, and the ball,
The sword, the mace, the crown imperial,
The intertissued robe of gold and pearl,
249 The farcèd title running 'fore the king,
The throne he sits on, nor the tide of pomp
251 That beats upon the high shore of this world –
No, not all these, thrice-gorgeous ceremony,
Not all these, laid in bed majestical,

222 *wringing* suffering **225** *ceremony* royal pomp **231** *soul of adoration* i.e. true essence of, or reason for, worship **241** *flexure* bowing **245** *find thee* find thee out, expose thee **246** *balm* consecrated oil used in coronation **249** *farcèd* stuffed, padded; *the king* i.e. the king's name **251** *high shore* i.e. sea cliffs (impervious to tides)

Can sleep so soundly as the wretched slave,
Who, with a body filled, and vacant mind,
Gets him to rest, crammed with distressful bread;
Never sees horrid night, the child of hell;
But like a lackey, from the rise to set,
Sweats in the eye of Phoebus, and all night
Sleeps in Elysium; next day after dawn,
Doth rise and help Hyperion to his horse;
And follows so the ever-running year
With profitable labor to his grave;
And but for ceremony, such a wretch,
Winding up days with toil and nights with sleep,
Had the forehand and vantage of a king.
The slave, a member of the country's peace,
Enjoys it; but in gross brain little wots
What watch the king keeps to maintain the peace,
Whose hours the peasant best advantages.

Enter Erpingham.

ERPINGHAM
My lord, your nobles, jealous of your absence,
Seek through your camp to find you.

KING
Good old knight,
Collect them all together at my tent.
I'll be before thee.

ERPINGHAM
I shall do't, my lord. *Exit.*

KING
O God of battles, steel my soldiers' hearts,
Possess them not with fear! Take from them now
The sense of reck'ning, if th' opposèd numbers
Pluck their hearts from them. Not to-day, O Lord,
O, not to-day, think not upon the fault
My father made in compassing the crown!

256 *distressful* i.e. hard-earned (?) 258 *lackey* constant attendant 259 *Sweats . . . Phoebus* i.e. works in sight of the sun 261 *Hyperion* charioteer of the sun 267 *member* sharer 269 *watch* wakeful guard 270 *advantages* profits 271 *jealous of* concerned about 277 *sense of reck'ning* ability to count 280 *compassing* obtaining

281 I Richard's body have interrèd new;
And on it have bestowed more contrite tears
Than from it issued forcèd drops of blood.
Five hundred poor I have in yearly pay,
Who twice a day their withered hands hold up
286 Toward heaven to pardon blood;
287 And I have built two chantries,
288 Where the sad and solemn priests sing still
For Richard's soul. More will I do:
Though all that I can do is nothing worth,
291 Since that my penitence comes after all,
Imploring pardon.

Enter Gloucester.

GLOUCESTER
My liege!

KING
My brother Gloucester's voice. Ay.
I know thy errand; I will go with thee.
The day, my friends, and all things stay for me. *Exeunt.*

*

IV, ii *Enter the Dauphin, Orleans, Rambures, and Beaumont.*

ORLEANS
The sun doth gild our armor. Up, my lords!
2 DAUPHIN Monte, cheval! My horse, varlet lacquais! Ha!
ORLEANS O brave spirit!
4 DAUPHIN Via les eaux et terre!

281 *new* anew 286 *blood* sinful flesh (?), the spilling of blood (?) 287 *chantries* chapels where masses are celebrated for the souls of the dead 288 *still* continuously 291 *Since that* i.e. as shown by the fact that

IV, ii The French camp s.d. *Beaumont* (a 'ghost' character, mute and appearing only in this one stage direction) 2 *Monte, cheval* soar, horse (cf. III, vii, 11–16); *varlet lacquais* rascal groom 4 *Via . . . terre* away waters and earth (i.e. streams and solid ground)

ORLEANS Rien puis les air et feu?
DAUPHIN Cieux! cousin Orleans.

Enter Constable.

Now, my Lord Constable?

CONSTABLE
Hark how our steeds for present service neigh!

DAUPHIN
Mount them and make incision in their hides,
That their hot blood may spin in English eyes
And dout them with superfluous courage, ha!

RAMBURES
What, will you have them weep our horses' blood?
How shall we then behold their natural tears?

Enter Messenger.

MESSENGER
The English are embattled, you French peers.

CONSTABLE
To horse, you gallant princes! straight to horse!
Do but behold yond poor and starvèd band,
And your fair show shall suck away their souls,
Leaving them but the shales and husks of men.
There is not work enough for all our hands,
Scarce blood enough in all their sickly veins
To give each naked curtle-axe a stain
That our French gallants shall to-day draw out
And sheathe for lack of sport. Let us but blow on them,
The vapor of our valor will o'erturn them.
'Tis positive 'gainst all exceptions, lords,
That our superfluous lackeys and our peasants,
Who in unnecessary action swarm

5 *Rien . . . feu?* not also air and fire? (Orleans jestingly takes the Dauphin's '*eaux*' and '*terre*' to refer to two of the four elements over which his horse will soar; and asks if it will not also soar above the realms of air and fire) 6 *Cieux* the heavens (to which, in the old cosmology, the realm of fire extended; the Dauphin has converted the joke into serious hyperbole) 11 *dout* extinguish; *superfluous courage* i.e. blood we can spare 18 *shales* shells 21 *curtle-axe* cutlass 25 *exceptions* objections

About our squares of battle, were enow
To purge this field of such a hilding foe,
Though we upon this mountain's basis by
Took stand for idle speculation:
But that our honors must not. What's to say?
A very little little let us do,
And all is done. Then let the trumpets sound
The tucket sonance and the note to mount;
For our approach shall so much dare the field
That England shall couch down in fear and yield.

Enter Grandpré.

GRANDPRÉ

Why do you stay so long, my lords of France?
Yond island carrions, desperate of their bones,
Ill-favoredly become the morning field.
Their ragged curtains poorly are let loose,
And our air shakes them passing scornfully.
Big Mars seems bankrout in their beggared host
And faintly through a rusty beaver peeps.
The horsemen sit like fixèd candlesticks
With torch-staves in their hand; and their poor jades
Lob down their heads, dropping the hides and hips,
The gum down roping from their pale-dead eyes,
And in their pale dull mouths the gimmaled bit
Lies foul with chawed grass, still and motionless;
And their executors, the knavish crows,
Fly o'er them all, impatient for their hour.
Description cannot suit itself in words
To demonstrate the life of such a battle
In life so lifeless as it shows itself.

29 *hilding* worthless 30 *mountain's basis by* i.e. nearby foothill 31 *speculation* viewing 35 *tucket sonance* trumpet call 36 *dare* daze (as the hawk terrifies its prey) 39 *carrions* cadavers; *desperate* despairing 41 *curtains* flags 43 *bankrout* bankrupt 44 *beaver* visor 46 *torch-staves* tapers 47 *Lob* droop 48 *roping* (cf. III, v, 23) 49 *gimmaled* jointed 51 *executors* disposers of the remains 55 *In life* in actuality

CONSTABLE
They have said their prayers, and they stay for death. 56

DAUPHIN
Shall we go send them dinners and fresh suits
And give their fasting horses provender,
And after fight with them ?

CONSTABLE
I stay but for my guard. On to the field ! 60
I will the banner from a trumpet take 61
And use it for my haste. Come, come away !
The sun is high, and we outwear the day. *Exeunt.* 63

*

IV, iii

Enter Gloucester, Bedford, Exeter, Erpingham with all his Host, Salisbury, and Westmoreland.

GLOUCESTER
Where is the king ?

BEDFORD
The king himself is rode to view their battle. 2

WESTMORELAND
Of fighting men they have full three-score thousand.

EXETER
There's five to one ; besides, they all are fresh.

SALISBURY
God's arm strike with us ! 'Tis a fearful odds.
God bye you, princes all ; I'll to my charge.
If we no more meet till we meet in heaven,
Then joyfully, my noble Lord of Bedford,
My dear Lord Gloucester, and my good Lord Exeter,
And my kind kinsman, warriors all, adieu !

BEDFORD
Farewell, good Salisbury, and good luck go with thee !

56 *stay* wait **60** *guard* (including color-bearer) **61** *trumpet* trumpeter
63 *outwear* waste
IV, iii The English camp **2** *battle* army

EXETER
Farewell, kind lord: fight valiantly to-day;
And yet I do thee wrong to mind thee of it,
For thou art framed of the firm truth of valor.
[Exit Salisbury.]

BEDFORD
He is as full of valor as of kindness,
Princely in both.
Enter the King.

WESTMORELAND O that we now had here
But one ten thousand of those men in England
That do no work to-day!

KING What's he that wishes so?
My cousin Westmoreland? No, my fair cousin.
If we are marked to die, we are enow
To do our country loss; and if to live,
The fewer men, the greater share of honor.
God's will! I pray thee wish not one man more.
By Jove, I am not covetous for gold,
Nor care I who doth feed upon my cost;
It yearns me not if men my garments wear;
Such outward things dwell not in my desires:
But if it be a sin to covet honor,
I am the most offending soul alive.
No, faith, my coz, wish not a man from England.
God's peace! I would not lose so great an honor
As one man more methinks would share from me
For the best hope I have. O, do not wish one more!
Rather proclaim it, Westmoreland, through my host,
That he which hath no stomach to this fight,
Let him depart; his passport shall be made,
And crowns for convoy put into his purse.
We would not die in that man's company
That fears his fellowship to die with us.

14 *framed . . . truth* i.e. made of the authentic stuff **20–21** *enow To do* enough to cause **26** *yearns* moves, grieves **30** *coz* cousin, kinsman **37** *convoy* transport **39** *fellowship* i.e. fraternal right

This day is called the Feast of Crispian.
He that outlives this day, and comes safe home,
Will stand a-tiptoe when this day is namèd
And rouse him at the name of Crispian.
He that shall see this day, and live old age,
Will yearly on the vigil feast his neighbors
And say, 'To-morrow is Saint Crispian.'
Then will he strip his sleeve and show his scars,
[And say, 'These wounds I had on Crispin's day.']
Old men forget; yet all shall be forgot,
But he'll remember, with advantages,
What feats he did that day. Then shall our names,
Familiar in his mouth as household words –
Harry the King, Bedford and Exeter,
Warwick and Talbot, Salisbury and Gloucester –
Be in their flowing cups freshly remember'd.
This story shall the good man teach his son;
And Crispin Crispian shall ne'er go by,
From this day to the ending of the world,
But we in it shall be rememberèd –
We few, we happy few, we band of brothers;
For he to-day that sheds his blood with me
Shall be my brother. Be he ne'er so vile, 62
This day shall gentle his condition; 63
And gentlemen in England now abed
Shall think themselves accursed they were not here,
And hold their manhoods cheap whiles any speaks
That fought with us upon Saint Crispin's day.

Enter Salisbury.

SALISBURY

My sovereign lord, bestow yourself with speed.
The French are bravely in their battles set
And will with all expedience charge on us.

40 *Feast of Crispian* October 25 (the brothers Crispianus and Crispinus were martyred A.D. 487; they became the patron saints of shoemakers) **50** *advantages* i.e. embellishments **62** *vile* low-born **63** *gentle his condition* i.e. achieve gentility **70** *expedience* expedition

KING
All things are ready, if our minds be so.
WESTMORELAND
Perish the man whose mind is backward now!
KING
Thou dost not wish more help from England, coz?
WESTMORELAND
God's will, my liege! would you and I alone,
Without more help, could fight this royal battle!
KING
Why, now thou hast unwished five thousand men!
Which likes me better than to wish us one.
You know your places. God be with you all!
Tucket. Enter Montjoy.
MONTJOY
Once more I come to know of thee, King Harry,
If for thy ransom thou wilt now compound,
Before thy most assurèd overthrow;
For certainly thou art so near the gulf
83 Thou needs must be englutted. Besides, in mercy,
84 The Constable desires thee thou wilt mind
Thy followers of repentance, that their souls
May make a peaceful and a sweet retire
From all these fields, where (wretches!) their poor bodies
Must lie and fester.
KING
Who hath sent thee now?
MONTJOY
The Constable of France.
KING
I pray thee bear my former answer back:
91 Bid them achieve me, and then sell my bones.
Good God! why should they mock poor fellows thus?
The man that once did sell the lion's skin
While the beast lived, was killed with hunting him.
A many of our bodies shall no doubt

80 *compound* come to terms 83 *englutted* swallowed up 84 *mind* remind
91 *achieve* win, capture

Find native graves; upon the which, I trust, 96
Shall witness live in brass of this day's work;
And those that leave their valiant bones in France,
Dying like men, though buried in your dunghills,
They shall be famed; for there the sun shall greet them
And draw their honors reeking up to heaven, 101
Leaving their earthly parts to choke your clime,
The smell whereof shall breed a plague in France.
Mark then abounding valor in our English,
That, being dead, like to the bullet's crasing, 105
Break out into a second course of mischief,
Killing in relapse of mortality. 107
Let me speak proudly. Tell the Constable
We are but warriors for the working day. 109
Our gayness and our gilt are all besmirched
With rainy marching in the painful field. 111
There's not a piece of feather in our host – 112
Good argument, I hope, we will not fly –
And time hath worn us into slovenry.
But, by the mass, our hearts are in the trim;
And my poor soldiers tell me, yet ere night
They'll be in fresher robes, or they will pluck 117
The gay new coats o'er the French soldiers' heads
And turn them out of service. If they do this, 119
As, if God please, they shall, my ransom then
Will soon be levied. Herald, save thou thy labor. 121
Come thou no more for ransom, gentle herald.
They shall have none, I swear, but these my joints;
Which if they have as I will leave 'em them,
Shall yield them little, tell the Constable.

96 *native* i.e. English 96–97 *upon . . . work* i.e. bearing bronze tablets commemorating their deeds at Agincourt 101 *reeking* breathing 105 *crasing* grazing, rebounding 107 *in . . . mortality* i.e. while in the process of decaying 109 *warriors . . . day* i.e. workaday or commonplace soldiers 111 *painful* arduous 112 *piece of feather* decorative plume 117 *in fresher robes* i.e. new-garbed in heaven 119 *turn . . . service* i.e. dismiss them stripped of their livery 121 *levied* collected (from the French themselves)

MONTJOY
I shall, King Harry. And so fare thee well.
Thou never shalt hear herald any more. *Exit.*

KING
I fear thou wilt once more come again for a ransom.

Enter York.

YORK
My lord, most humbly on my knee I beg
The leading of the vaward.

KING
Take it, brave York. Now, soldiers, march away;
And how thou pleasest, God, dispose the day! *Exeunt.*

*

IV, iv *Alarum. Excursions. Enter Pistol, French Soldier, Boy.*

PISTOL Yield, cur!

FRENCH SOLDIER Je pense que vous estes le gentilhomme de bon qualité.

PISTOL Qualtitie calmie custure me! Art thou a gentleman? What is thy name? Discuss.

FRENCH SOLDIER O Seigneur Dieu!

PISTOL
O Signieur Dew should be a gentleman.
Perpend my words, O Signieur Dew, and mark.
O Signieur Dew, thou diest on point of fox,
Except, O signieur, thou do give to me
Egregious ransom.

128 *again* (perhaps an intrusion in the text) 130 *vaward* vanguard
IV, iv The battlefield of Agincourt 2–3 *Je . . . qualité* I think you are a gentleman of rank 4 *Qualtitie . . . me* (gibberish, echoing *qualité* in l. 3, together with refrain of a popular ballad, 'Callen o custare me'; the refrain itself derives from an Irish line '*Cailin ó chois tSúire me*, meaning 'I am a girl from beside the Suir') 5 *Discuss* declare 8 *Perpend* consider 9 *fox* sword (derived from trademark of a famous swordmaker) 11 *Egregious* extraordinary

FRENCH SOLDIER O, prenez miséricorde! ayez pitié de moi! 12

PISTOL
Moy shall not serve. I will have forty moys,
Or I will fetch thy rim out at thy throat 14
In drops of crimson blood.

FRENCH SOLDIER Est-il impossible d'eschapper le force de ton bras? 16

PISTOL Brass, cur?
Thou damnèd and luxurious mountain goat, 19
Offer'st me brass?

FRENCH SOLDIER O, pardonnez-moi!

PISTOL
Say'st thou me so? Is that a ton of moys?
Come hither, boy; ask me this slave in French
What is his name.

BOY Escoute. Comment estes-vous appelé? 25

FRENCH SOLDIER Monsieur le Fer.

BOY He says his name is Master Fer.

PISTOL Master Fer? I'll fer him, and firk him, and ferret him! Discuss the same in French unto him. 28

BOY I do not know the French for 'fer,' and 'ferret,' and 'firk.'

PISTOL
Bid him prepare, for I will cut his throat.

FRENCH SOLDIER Que dit-il, monsieur? 33

BOY Il me commande de vous dire que vous faites vous 34
prest; car ce soldat ici est disposé tout asture de couper 35
vostre gorge.

PISTOL
Owy, cuppe le gorge, permafoy,

12–13 *O . . . moi* O, have mercy! take pity on me 14 *rim* belly-lining 16–17 *Est-il . . . bras* is it impossible to escape the strength of your arm 19 *luxurious* lecherous 25 *Escoute . . . appelé* listen, what is your name 28 *firk* beat; *ferret* worry 33 *Que . . . monsieur* what does he say, sir 34–36 *Il . . . gorge* he bids me tell you to prepare, for this soldier is disposed to cut your throat at once 35 *asture* i.e. '*à cette heure*,' at once

Peasant, unless thou give me crowns, brave crowns,
O'er-mangled shalt thou be by this my sword.

FRENCH SOLDIER O, je vous supplie, pour l'amour de Dieu, me pardonner! Je suis le gentilhomme de bon maison. Gardez ma vie, et je vous donnerai deux cents escus.

PISTOL
What are his words?

BOY He prays you to save his life. He is a gentleman of a good house, and for his ransom he will give you two hundred crowns.

PISTOL
Tell him my fury shall abate, and I
The crowns will take.

49 FRENCH SOLDIER Petit monsieur, que dit-il?

50 BOY Encore qu'il est contre son jurement de pardonner aucun prisonnier; néantmoins, pour les escus que vous l'avez promis, il est content de vous donner le liberté, le franchisement.

FRENCH SOLDIER Sur mes genoux je vous donne mille remercîmens; et je m'estime heureux que j'ai tombé entre les mains d'un chevalier, je pense, le plus brave, vaillant, et très-distingué seigneur d'Angleterre.

PISTOL
Expound unto me, boy.

BOY He gives you, upon his knees, a thousand thanks; and he esteems himself happy that he hath fall'n into the hands of one, as he thinks, the most brave, valorous, and thrice-worthy signieur of England.

PISTOL
63 As I suck blood, I will some mercy show!
Follow me. *[Exit.]*

BOY Suivez-vous le grand capitaine. *[Exit French Soldier.]*

49 *Petit . . . dit-il* small sir, what says he 50–53 *Encore . . . franchisement* although it is against his oath to pardon any prisoner, still for the crowns you have promised he is willing to give you liberty, freedom 63 *suck blood* (cf. II, iii, 50–51)

I did never know so full a voice issue from so empty a heart; but the saying is true, 'The empty vessel makes the greatest sound.' Bardolph and Nym had ten times more valor than this roaring devil i' th' old play that 69
every one may pare his nails with a wooden dagger; and they are both hanged; and so would this be, if he durst steal anything adventurously. I must stay with the lackeys with the luggage of our camp. The French might have a good prey of us, if he knew of it; for there is none to guard it but boys. *Exit.*

Enter Constable, Orleans, Bourbon, Dauphin, and Rambures. IV, v

CONSTABLE O diable!

ORLEANS O Seigneur! le jour est perdu, tout est perdu! 2

DAUPHIN

Mort de ma vie! all is confounded, all! 3
Reproach and everlasting shame
Sits mocking in our plumes.

A short alarum.

O meschante fortune! Do not run away. 6

CONSTABLE

Why, all our ranks are broke.

DAUPHIN

O perdurable shame! Let's stab ourselves. 8
Be these the wretches that we played at dice for?

ORLEANS

Is this the king we sent to for his ransom?

BOURBON

Shame, and eternal shame! nothing but shame!
Let us die in honor. Once more back again!
And he that will not follow Bourbon now,
Let him go hence, and with his cap in hand

69 *roaring devil* i.e. the devil or Vice in the old morality plays, sometimes subjected to the indignity of having his claws pared

IV, v 2 *O . . . perdu* O Lord! the day is lost, all is lost 3 *Mort . . . vie* death of my life; *confounded* ruined 6 *O . . . fortune* O tainted Fortune 8 *perdurable* enduring

Like a base pander hold the chamber door
Whilst by a slave, no gentler than my dog,
His fairest daughter is contaminated.

CONSTABLE

18 Disorder, that hath spoiled us, friend us now!
Let us on heaps go offer up our lives.

ORLEANS

We are enow yet living in the field
To smother up the English in our throngs,
If any order might be thought upon.

BOURBON

The devil take order now! I'll to the throng.
Let life be short; else shame will be too long. *Exeunt.*

IV, vi *Alarum. Enter the King and his Train, [Exeter, and others,] with Prisoners.*

KING

Well have we done, thrice-valiant countrymen;
But all's not done, yet keep the French the field.

EXETER

The Duke of York commends him to your majesty.

KING

Lives he, good uncle? Thrice within this hour
I saw him down; thrice up again and fighting.
From helmet to the spur all blood he was.

EXETER

In which array, brave soldier, doth he lie,
8 Larding the plain; and by his bloody side,
Yoke-fellow to his honor-owing wounds,
The noble Earl of Suffolk also lies.
11 Suffolk first died; and York, all haggled over,
Comes to him, where in gore he lay insteepèd,
And takes him by the beard, kisses the gashes
That bloodily did yawn upon his face,
And cries aloud, 'Tarry, my cousin Suffolk!
My soul shall thine keep company to heaven.

18 *spoiled* despoiled, ruined

IV, vi 8 *Larding* fattening, fertilizing 11 *haggled* hacked

Tarry, sweet soul, for mine, then fly abreast;
As in this glorious and well-foughten field
We kept together in our chivalry!'
Upon these words I came and cheered him up.
He smiled me in the face, raught me his hand, 21
And with a feeble gripe, says, 'Dear my lord,
Commend my service to my sovereign.'
So did he turn, and over Suffolk's neck
He threw his wounded arm and kissed his lips;
And so, espoused to death, with blood he sealed
A testament of noble-ending love.
The pretty and sweet manner of it forced
Those waters from me which I would have stopped;
But I had not so much of man in me,
And all my mother came into mine eyes 31
And gave me up to tears.

KING I blame you not;
For hearing this, I must perforce compound 33
With mistful eyes, or they will issue too. *Alarum.* 34
But hark! what new alarum is this same?
The French have reinforced their scattered men.
Then every soldier kill his prisoners!
Give the word through. *Exit [with others].*

*

Enter Fluellen and Gower. IV, vii

FLUELLEN Kill the poys and the luggage? 'Tis expressly against the law of arms. 'Tis as arrant a piece of knavery, mark you now, as can be offert. In your conscience, now, is it not?

GOWER 'Tis certain there's not a boy left alive; and the cowardly rascals that ran from the battle ha' done this slaughter. Besides, they have burned and carried away

21 *raught* reached **31** *mother* i.e. womanly tenderness **33** *compound* come to terms **34** *mistful* tearful; *issue* run (tears)
IV, vii The battlefield of Agincourt

all that was in the king's tent; wherefore the king most
worthily hath caused every soldier to cut his prisoner's
throat. O, 'tis a gallant king!

11 FLUELLEN Ay, he was porn at Monmouth, Captain
Gower. What call you the town's name where Alexander the Pig was born.

GOWER Alexander the Great.

FLUELLEN Why, I pray you, is not 'pig' great? The pig,
or the great, or the mighty, or the huge, or the magnanimous are all one reckonings, save the phrase is a
17 little variations.

GOWER I think Alexander the Great was born in Macedon.
His father was called Philip of Macedon, as I take it.

FLUELLEN I think it is in Macedon where Alexander is
porn. I tell you, captain, if you look in the maps of the
orld, I warrant you sall find, in the comparisons between Macedon and Monmouth, that the situations,
24 look you, is poth alike. There is a river in Macedon, and
there is also moreover a river at Monmouth. It is called
Wye at Monmouth; but it is out of my prains what is the
name of the other river. But 'tis all one; 'tis alike as my
fingers is to my fingers, and there is salmons in poth. If
you mark Alexander's life well, Harry of Monmouth's
30 life is come after it indifferent well; for there is figures
in all things. Alexander, God knows and you know, in
his rages, and his furies, and his wraths, and his cholers,
and his moods, and his displeasures, and his indignations, and also being a little intoxicates in his prains, did,
in his ales and his angers, look you, kill his best friend,
35 Cleitus.

GOWER Our king is not like him in that. He never killed
any of his friends.

11 *Monmouth* i.e. in Wales 17 *variations* i.e. altered 24 *river* (there follows a parody of rhetorical 'comparisons') 30 *is come after* i.e. resembles; *figures* comparisons 35 *Cleitus* friend of Alexander, slain in drunken rage for praising Philip

FLUELLEN It is not well done, mark you now, to take the
tales out of my mouth ere it is made and finished. I speak
but in the figures and comparisons of it. As Alexander
killed his friend Cleitus, being in his ales and his cups,
so also Harry Monmouth, being in his right wits and his
good judgments, turned away the fat knight with the
great pelly doublet. He was full of jests, and gipes, and 44
knaveries, and mocks. I have forgot his name.

GOWER Sir John Falstaff.

FLUELLEN That is he. I'll tell you there is good men porn at Monmouth.

GOWER Here comes his majesty.

Alarum. Enter King Harry and Bourbon, [Warwick, Gloucester, Exeter, and Herald,] with Prisoners. Flourish.

KING

I was not angry since I came to France
Until this instant. Take a trumpet, herald; 51
Ride thou unto the horsemen on yond hill.
If they will fight with us, bid them come down
Or void the field. They do offend our sight. 54
If they'll do neither, we will come to them
And make them skirr away as swift as stones 56
Enforcèd from the old Assyrian slings. 57
Besides, we'll cut the throats of those we have;
And not a man of them that we shall take
Shall taste our mercy. Go and tell them so.

[Exeunt Herald and Gower.]

Enter Montjoy.

EXETER

Here comes the herald of the French, my liege.

GLOUCESTER

His eyes are humbler than they used to be.

KING

How now? What means this, herald? Know'st thou not

44 *great pelly* stuffed belly; *gipes* japes 51 *trumpet* trumpeter 54 *void* leave, depart from 56 *skirr* scurry 57 *Enforcèd* driven

That I have fined these bones of mine for ransom?
Com'st thou again for ransom?

HERALD No, great king.
I come to thee for charitable license
That we may wander o'er this bloody field
To book our dead, and then to bury them;
To sort our nobles from our common men.
For many of our princes, woe the while!
Lie drowned and soaked in mercenary blood.
So do our vulgar drench their peasant limbs
In blood of princes, and the wounded steeds
Fret fetlock-deep in gore and with wild rage
Yerk out their armèd heels at their dead masters,
Killing them twice. O, give us leave, great king,
To view the field in safety and dispose
Of their dead bodies!

KING I tell thee truly, herald,
I know not if the day be ours or no;
For yet a many of your horsemen peer
And gallop o'er the field.

HERALD The day is yours.

KING
Praisèd be God and not our strength for it!
What is this castle called that stands hard by?

HERALD
They call it Agincourt.

KING
Then call we this the field of Agincourt,
Fought on the day of Crispin Crispianus.

FLUELLEN Your grandfather of famous memory, an't please your majesty, and your great-uncle Edward the Plack Prince of Wales, as I have read in the chronicles, fought a most prave pattle here in France.

KING They did, Fluellen.

FLUELLEN Your majesty says very true. If your majesties

64 *fined* pledged 68 *book* register 71 *mercenary blood* blood of hired soldiers 75 *Yerk* kick 80 *peer* appear

is remembʼred of it, the Welshmen did good service in a garden where leeks did grow, wearing leeks in their Monmouth caps; which your majesty know to this hour is an honorable padge of the service; and I do believe your majesty takes no scorn to wear the leek upon Saint Tavy's day.

KING
I wear it for a memorable honor;
For I am Welsh, you know, good countryman.

FLUELLEN All the water in Wye cannot wash your majesty's Welsh plood out of your pody, I can tell you that. God pless it and preserve it, as long as it pleases his grace, and his majesty too!

KING Thanks, good my countryman.

FLUELLEN By Cheshu, I am your majesty's countryman, I care not who know it! I will confess it to all the orld. I need not to be ashamed of your majesty, praised be God, so long as your majesty is an honest man.

KING
God keep me so! Our heralds go with him.
Enter Williams.
Bring me just notice of the numbers dead
On both our parts. *[Exeunt Heralds with Montjoy.]*
Call yonder fellow hither.

EXETER Soldier, you must come to the king.

KING Soldier, why wear'st thou that glove in thy cap?

WILLIAMS An't please your majesty, 'tis the gage of one that I should fight withal, if he be alive.

KING An Englishman?

WILLIAMS An't please your majesty, a rascal that swaggered with me last night; who, if 'a live and ever dare to challenge this glove, I have sworn to take him a box o' th' ear; or if I can see my glove in his cap, which he swore, as he was a soldier, he would wear if alive, I will strike it out soundly.

95 *Monmouth caps* tall tapering hats without brims

KING What think you, Captain Fluellen? Is it fit this soldier keep his oath?

FLUELLEN He is a craven and a villain else, an't please your majesty, in my conscience.

KING It may be his enemy is a gentleman of great sort,
129 quite from the answer of his degree.

FLUELLEN Though he be as good a gentleman as the
devil is, as Lucifer and Belzebub himself, it is necessary,
look your grace, that he keep his vow and his oath. If he
be perjured, see you now, his reputation is as arrant a
134 villain and a jack sauce as ever his plack shoe trod upon
God's ground and his earth, in my conscience, law!

KING Then keep thy vow, sirrah, when thou meet'st the fellow.

WILLIAMS So I will, my liege, as I live.

KING Who serv'st thou under?

WILLIAMS Under Captain Gower, my liege.

FLUELLEN Gower is a good captain and is good knowl-
142 edge and literatured in the wars.

KING Call him hither to me, soldier.

WILLIAMS I will, my liege. *Exit.*

KING Here, Fluellen; wear thou this favor for me and stick it in thy cap. When Alençon and myself were down together, I plucked this glove from his helm. If any man challenge this, he is a friend to Alençon and an enemy to our person. If thou encounter any such, apprehend him, an thou dost me love.

FLUELLEN Your grace doo's me as great honors as can be
desired in the hearts of his subjects. I would fain see the
153 man, that has but two legs, that shall find himself aggriefed at this glove, that is all. But I would fain see it
once, an please God of his grace that I might see.

KING Know'st thou Gower?

FLUELLEN He is my dear friend, an please you.

129 *from . . . degree* above responding to a challenge from one of his rank 134 *as ever* as sure as 142 *literatured* well-read, learned 153 *aggriefed* aggrieved, incensed

KING Pray thee go seek him and bring him to my tent.
FLUELLEN I will fetch him *Exit.*
KING
My Lord of Warwick, and my brother Gloucester,
Follow Fluellen closely at the heels.
The glove which I have given him for a favor
May haply purchase him a box o' th' ear;
It is the soldier's. I by bargain should
Wear it myself. Follow, good cousin Warwick.
If that the soldier strike him – as I judge
By his blunt bearing, he will keep his word –
Some sudden mischief may arise of it;
For I do know Fluellen valiant,
And, touched with choler, hot as gunpowder,
And quickly will return an injury.
Follow, and see there be no harm between them.
Go you with me, uncle of Exeter *Exeunt.*

*

Enter Gower and Williams. IV, viii

WILLIAMS I warrant it is to knight you, captain
Enter Fluellen.

FLUELLEN God's will and his pleasure, captain, I beseech you now, come apace to the king. There is more good toward you peradventure than is in your knowledge to dream of

WILLIAMS Sir, know you this glove?
FLUELLEN Know the glove? I know the glove is a glove.
WILLIAMS I know this; and thus I challenge it.
Strikes him.

FLUELLEN 'Sblood! an arrant traitor as any's in the universal orld, or in France, or in England!

GOWER How now, sir? You villain!
WILLIAMS Do you think I'll be forsworn?

162 *favor* token 170 *touched . . . choler* i.e. quick-tempered
IV, viii The English camp

FLUELLEN Stand away, Captain Gower. I will give treason his payment into plows, I warrant you.

WILLIAMS I am no traitor.

FLUELLEN That's a lie in thy throat. I charge you in his majesty's name apprehend him. He's a friend of the Duke Alençon's.

Enter Warwick and Gloucester.

WARWICK How now, how now? What's the matter?

FLUELLEN My Lord of Warwick, here is, praised be God for it, a most contagious treason come to light, look you, as you shall desire in a summer's day. Here is his majesty.

Enter King and Exeter.

KING How now? What's the matter?

FLUELLEN My liege, here is a villain and a traitor that, look your grace, has struck the glove which your majesty is take out of the helmet of Alençon.

WILLIAMS My liege, this was my glove, here is the fellow of it; and he that I gave it to in change promised to wear it in his cap. I promised to strike him if he did. I met this man with my glove in his cap, and I have been as good as my word.

FLUELLEN Your majesty hear now, saving your majesty's manhood, what an arrant, rascally, peggarly, lousy knave it is! I hope your majesty is pear me testimony and witness, and will avouchment, that this is the glove of Alençon that your majesty is give me, in your conscience, now.

KING
Give me thy glove, soldier. Look, here is the fellow of it.
'Twas I indeed thou promisèd'st to strike;
And thou hast given me most bitter terms.

FLUELLEN An please your majesty, let his neck answer for it, if there is any martial law in the orld.

12 *his* its 20 *contagious* noxious 26 *fellow* mate 27 *change* exchange
34 *avouchment* i.e. avouch

KING How canst thou make me satisfaction?

WILLIAMS All offenses, my lord, come from the heart. Never came any from mine that might offend your majesty.

KING It was ourself thou didst abuse.

WILLIAMS Your majesty came not like yourself. You appeared to me but as a common man; witness the night, your garments, your lowliness. And what your highness suffered under that shape, I beseech you take it for your own fault, and not mine; for had you been as I took you for, I made no offense. Therefore I beseech your highness pardon me.

KING
Here, uncle Exeter, fill this glove with crowns
And give it to this fellow. Keep it, fellow,
And wear it for an honor in thy cap
Till I do challenge it. Give him the crowns;
And captain, you must needs be friends with him.

FLUELLEN By this day and this light, the fellow has mettle enough in his pelly. Hold, there is twelve pence for you; and I pray you to serve God, and keep you out of prawls, and prabbles, and quarrels, and dissensions, and, I warrant you, it is the petter for you.

WILLIAMS I will none of your money.

FLUELLEN It is with a good will. I can tell you it will serve you to mend your shoes. Come, wherefore should you be so pashful? Your shoes is not so good. 'Tis a good silling, I warrant you, or I will change it.

Enter [an English] Herald.

KING
Now, herald, are the dead numb'red?

HERALD
Here is the number of the slaught'red French.
[Gives a paper.]

48 *lowliness* i.e. humble bearing 58 *mettle* i.e. courage

KING

70 What prisoners of good sort are taken, uncle?

EXETER

Charles Duke of Orleans, nephew to the king;
John Duke of Bourbon and Lord Bouciqualt:
Of other lords and barons, knights and squires,
Full fifteen hundred, besides common men.

KING

This note doth tell me of ten thousand French
That in the field lie slain. Of princes, in this number,
77 And nobles bearing banners, there lie dead
One hundred twenty-six; added to these,
Of knights, esquires, and gallant gentlemen,
Eight thousand and four hundred; of the which,
Five hundred were but yesterday dubbed knights;
82 So that in these ten thousand they have lost
There are but sixteen hundred mercenaries;
The rest are princes, barons, lords, knights, squires,
And gentlemen of blood and quality.
The names of those their nobles that lie dead:
Charles Delabreth, High Constable of France;
Jacques of Chatillon, Admiral of France;
The master of the crossbows, Lord Rambures;
Great Master of France, the brave Sir Guichard Dauphin;
John Duke of Alençon; Anthony Duke of Brabant,
The brother to the Duke of Burgundy;
And Edward Duke of Bar; of lusty earls,
Grandpré and Roussi, Faulconbridge and Foix,
Beaumont and Marle, Vaudemont and Lestrale.
Here was a royal fellowship of death!
Where is the number of our English dead?
[Herald gives another paper.]
Edward the Duke of York, the Earl of Suffolk,

70 *good sort* high rank 77 *bearing banners* (cf. IV, ii, 61–62) 82 *ten thousand* (the mortality figures are from Hall and Holinshed; the modern estimate is about 7000)

Sir Richard Ketly, Davy Gam, esquire; 99
None else of name; and of all other men
But five-and-twenty. O God, thy arm was here! 101
And not to us, but to thy arm alone,
Ascribe we all! When, without stratagem,
But in plain shock and even play of battle,
Was ever known so great and little loss
On one part and on th' other? Take it, God, 106
For it is none but thine!

EXETER 'Tis wonderful!

KING
Come, go we in procession to the village;
And be it death proclaimèd through our host
To boast of this, or take that praise from God
Which is his only.

FLUELLEN Is it not lawful, an please your majesty, to tell how many is killed?

KING
Yes, captain; but with this acknowledgment,
That God fought for us.

FLUELLEN Yes, my conscience, he did us great good.

KING
Do we all holy rites.
Let there be sung 'Non nobis' and 'Te Deum,' 118
The dead with charity enclosed in clay,
And then to Calais; and to England then;
Where ne'er from France arrived more happy men. 121

Exeunt.

*

99 *Davy Gam* David ap Llewellyn **101** *five-and-twenty* (the figure given by Hall; the modern estimate is about 450) **106** *Take it* i.e. take the credit **118** *Non nobis* i.e. Psalm cxv, beginning in English 'Not unto us, O Lord, not unto us, but unto thy name give glory'; *Te Deum* song of thanksgiving beginning in English 'We praise thee, O God' **121** *happy* fortunate

V, Cho. *Enter Chorus.*

Vouchsafe to those that have not read the story
That I may prompt them; and of such as have,
I humbly pray them to admit th' excuse
Of time, of numbers, and due course of things
Which cannot in their huge and proper life
Be here presented. Now we bear the king
Toward Calais. Grant him there. There seen,
Heave him away upon your wingèd thoughts
Athwart the sea. Behold, the English beach
Pales in the flood with men, wives, and boys,
Whose shouts and claps outvoice the deep-mouthed sea,
Which, like a mighty whiffler 'fore the king,
Seems to prepare his way. So let him land,
And solemnly see him set on to London.
So swift a pace hath thought that even now
You may imagine him upon Blackheath;
Where that his lords desire him to have borne
His bruisèd helmet and his bended sword
Before him through the city. He forbids it,
Being free from vainness and self-glorious pride;
Giving full trophy, signal, and ostent
Quite from himself to God. But now behold,
In the quick forge and working-house of thought,
How London doth pour out her citizens!
The mayor and all his brethren in best sort,
Like to the senators of th' antique Rome,
With the plebeians swarming at their heels,
Go forth and fetch their conqu'ring Caesar in;
As, by a lower but by loving likelihood,
Were now the general of our gracious empress,

V, Cho. 3 *admit th'excuse* i.e. tolerate the treatment 10 *Pales* hems 12 *whiffler* member of an armed escort clearing the way for a procession 21 *signal, and ostent* token and show (of victory) 23 *quick . . . thought* i.e. nimble creative imagination 29 *lower . . . likelihood* i.e. less exalted but no less longed-for possibility 30 *general* i.e. Robert Devereux, Earl of Essex, whose inglorious campaign in Ireland ended in September, 1599

As in good time he may, from Ireland coming,
Bringing rebellion broachèd on his sword, 32
How many would the peaceful city quit
To welcome him! Much more, and much more cause,
Did they this Harry. Now in London place him;
As yet the lamentation of the French 36
Invites the King of England's stay at home;
The emperor's coming in behalf of France 38
To order peace between them; and omit
All the occurrences, whatever chanced,
Till Harry's back-return again to France.
There must we bring him; and myself have played 42
The interim, by rememb'ring you 'tis past. 43
Then brook abridgment; and your eyes advance, 44
After your thoughts, straight back again to France.

Exit.

Enter Fluellen and Gower. V, i

GOWER Nay, that's right. But why wear you your leek today? Saint Davy's day is past.

FLUELLEN There is occasions and causes why and wherefore in all things. I will tell you ass my friend, Captain
Gower. The rascally, scald, peggarly, lousy, pragging 5
knave, Pistol, which you and yourself and all the orld
know to be no petter than a fellow, look you now, of no 7
merits, he is come to me and prings me pread and salt
yesterday, look you, and pid me eat my leek. It was in a
place where I could not preed no contention with him; 10
but I will be so pold as to wear it in my cap till I see him once again, and then I will tell him a little piece of my desires.

32 *broachèd* impaled 36 *As . . . lamentation* while the continuing state of dejection 38 *emperor's coming* i.e. the Holy Roman Emperor Sigismund's mission to England in May, 1416 42–43 *played The interim* filled up the interval 43 *rememb'ring* reminding 44 *brook* put up with

V, i The English camp 5 *scald* scurvy 7 *fellow* i.e. groom 10 *preed* i.e. breed, foment

Enter Pistol.

GOWER Why, here he comes, swelling like a turkey cock.

FLUELLEN 'Tis no matter for his swellings nor his turkey cocks. God pless you, Aunchient Pistol! you scurvy, lousy knave, God pless you!

PISTOL

Ha! art thou bedlam? Dost thou thirst, base Trojan,
To have me fold up Parca's fatal web?
Hence! I am qualmish at the smell of leek.

FLUELLEN I beseech you heartily, scurvy, lousy knave, at my desires, and my requests, and my petitions, to eat, look you, this leek. Because, look you, you do not love it, nor your affections and your appetites and your disgestions doo's not agree with it, I would desire you to eat it.

PISTOL

Not for Cadwallader and all his goats.

FLUELLEN There is one goat for you. (*Strikes him.*) Will you be so good, scald knave, as eat it?

PISTOL

Base Trojan, thou shalt die!

FLUELLEN You say very true, scald knave, when God's will is. I will desire you to live in the meantime, and eat your victuals. Come, there is sauce for it. *[Strikes him.]* You called me yesterday mountain-squire; but I will make you to-day a squire of low degree. I pray you fall to. If you can mock a leek, you can eat a leek.

GOWER Enough, captain. You have astonished him.

FLUELLEN I say I will make him eat some part of my leek, or I will peat his pate four days. – Pite, I pray you. It is good for your green wound and your ploody coxcomb.

PISTOL Must I bite?

FLUELLEN Yes, certainly, and out of doubt, and out of question too, and ambiguities.

17 *bedlam* mad; *Trojan* roisterer 18 *fold . . . web* i.e. complete the design of the Parcae (Fates) by ending your life 25 *Cadwallader* (last of the British kings); *goats* (associated with Welsh poverty) 35 *astonished* dazed 38 *green* raw; *coxcomb* fool's scalp

PISTOL By this leek, I will most horribly revenge. I eat and eat, I swear.

FLUELLEN Eat, I pray you. Will you have some more sauce to your leek? There is not enough leek to swear by.

PISTOL Quiet thy cudgel, thou dost see I eat.

FLUELLEN Much good do you, scald knave, heartily. Nay, pray you throw none away, the skin is good for your proken coxcomb. When you take occasions to see leeks hereafter, I pray you mock at 'em; that is all.

PISTOL Good.

FLUELLEN Ay, leeks is good. Hold you, there is a groat to 52
heal your pate.

PISTOL Me a groat?

FLUELLEN Yes verily, and in truth you shall take it, or I have another leek in my pocket which you shall eat.

PISTOL
I take thy groat in earnest of revenge.

FLUELLEN If I owe you anything, I will pay you in cudgels. You shall be a woodmonger and buy nothing of me but cudgels. God bye you, and keep you, and heal your pate. *Exit.*

PISTOL
All hell shall stir for this!

GOWER Go, go. You are a counterfeit cowardly knave. Will you mock at an ancient tradition, begun upon an
honorable respect and won as a memorable trophy of 64
predeceased valor, and dare not avouch in your deeds any
of your words? I have seen you gleeking and galling at 66
this gentleman twice or thrice. You thought, because he could not speak English in the native garb, he could not therefore handle an English cudgel. You find it otherwise, and henceforth let a Welsh correction teach you a good English condition. Fare ye well. *Exit.*

PISTOL
Doth Fortune play the huswife with me now? 72

52 *groat* fourpenny piece 64 *respect* consideration 66 *gleeking and galling* gibing and scoffing 72 *huswife* hussy

73 News have I, that my Doll is dead i' th' spital
74 Of a malady of France;
And there my rendezvous is quite cut off.
Old I do wax, and from my weary limbs
Honor is cudgelled. Well, bawd I'll turn,
78 And something lean to cutpurse of quick hand.
To England will I steal, and there I'll steal;
And patches will I get unto these cudgelled scars
81 And swear I got them in the Gallia wars. *Exit.*

*

V, ii *Enter, at one door, King Henry, Exeter, Bedford, [Gloucester,] Warwick, [Westmoreland,] and other Lords; at another, Queen Isabel, the [French] King, the Duke of Burgundy, [the Princess Katherine, Alice,] and other French.*

KING HENRY
Peace to this meeting, wherefore we are met.
Unto our brother France and to our sister
Health and fair time of day. Joy and good wishes
To our most fair and princely cousin Katherine.
And as a branch and member of this royalty,
By whom this great assembly is contrived,
We do salute you, Duke of Burgundy.
And, princes French, and peers, health to you all.

FRANCE
Right joyous are we to behold your face,
Most worthy brother England. Fairly met.
So are you, princes English, every one.

QUEEN
So happy be the issue, brother England,

73 *Doll* (error for Nell); *spital* hospital 74 *malady of France* venereal disease 78 *something . . . hand* i.e. lean to quick-handed purse-cutting 81 *Gallia* French

V, ii Within the palace of the French king at Troyes 5 *royalty* royal family

Of this good day and of this gracious meeting
As we are now glad to behold your eyes –
Your eyes which hitherto have borne in them,
Against the French that met them in their bent,
The fatal balls of murdering basilisks. 17
The venom of such looks, we fairly hope,
Have lost their quality, and that this day
Shall change all griefs and quarrels into love.

KING HENRY
To cry amen to that, thus we appear.

QUEEN
You English princes all, I do salute you.

BURGUNDY
My duty to you both, on equal love,
Great Kings of France and England! That I have labored
With all my wits, my pains, and strong endeavors
To bring your most imperial majesties
Unto this bar and royal interview, 27
Your mightiness on both parts best can witness.
Since, then, my office hath so far prevailed
That, face to face and royal eye to eye,
You have congreeted, let it not disgrace me 31
If I demand before this royal view,
What rub or what impediment there is 33
Why that the naked, poor, and mangled Peace,
Dear nurse of arts, plenties, and joyful births,
Should not, in this best garden of the world,
Our fertile France, put up her lovely visage.
Alas, she hath from France too long been chased,
And all her husbandry doth lie on heaps,
Corrupting in it own fertility. 40
Her vine, the merry cheerer of the heart,
Unprunèd dies; her hedges even-pleachèd, 42
Like prisoners wildly overgrown with hair,

17 *basilisks* monsters which killed with a look; here, cannons 27 *bar* court of justice 31 *congreeted* greeted each other; *disgrace* ill become 33 *rub* obstacle 40 *it* its 42 *even-pleached* evenly pleated

44 Put forth disordered twigs; her fallow leas
The darnel, hemlock, and rank fumitory
46 Doth root upon, while that the coulter rusts
That should deracinate such savagery.
48 The even mead, that erst brought sweetly forth
The freckled cowslip, burnet, and green clover,
Wanting the scythe, all uncorrected, rank,
Conceives by idleness, and nothing teems
52 But hateful docks, rough thistles, kecksies, burrs,
Losing both beauty and utility.
And all our vineyards, fallows, meads, and hedges,
55 Defective in their natures, grow to wildness.
Even so our houses and ourselves and children
Have lost, or do not learn for want of time,
The sciences that should become our country;
But grow like savages, as soldiers will,
That nothing do but meditate on blood,
61 To swearing and stern looks, diffused attire,
And everything that seems unnatural.
63 Which to reduce into our former favor
You are assembled; and my speech entreats
65 That I may know the let why gentle Peace
Should not expel these inconveniences
And bless us with her former qualities.

KING HENRY

If, Duke of Burgundy, you would the peace
Whose want gives growth to th' imperfections
Which you have cited, you must buy that peace
With full accord to all our just demands;
72 Whose tenures and particular effects
You have, enscheduled briefly, in your hands.

BURGUNDY

The king hath heard them; to the which as yet

44 *leas* arable fields 40 *coulter* cutting wheel or blade in front of ploughshare 48 *erst* formerly 52 *kecksies* kexes, dry stems 55 *Defective* i.e. fallen, blighted by original sin 61 *diffused* disordered 63 *reduce* lead back; *favor* appearance 65 *let* hindrance 72 *tenures* gist

There is no answer made.

KING HENRY Well then, the peace,
Which you before so urged, lies in his answer.

FRANCE
I have but with a cursitory eye 77
O'erglanced the articles. Pleaseth your grace
To appoint some of your Council presently
To sit with us once more, with better heed
To resurvey them, we will suddenly
Pass our accept and peremptory answer. 82

KING HENRY
Brother, we shall. Go, uncle Exeter,
And brother Clarence, and you, brother Gloucester,
Warwick, and Huntingdon, go with the king;
And take with you free power to ratify,
Augment, or alter, as your wisdoms best
Shall see advantageable for our dignity,
Anything in or out of our demands,
And we'll consign thereto. Will you, fair sister, 90
Go with the princes or stay here with us?

QUEEN
Our gracious brother, I will go with them.
Happily a woman's voice may do some good 93
When articles too nicely urged be stood on. 94

KING HENRY
Yet leave our cousin Katherine here with us.
She is our capital demand, comprised 96
Within the fore-rank of our articles.

QUEEN
She hath good leave.

Exeunt omnes. Manent King [Henry] and Katherine [with the Gentlewoman Alice].

KING HENRY Fair Katherine, and most fair,
Will you vouchsafe to teach a soldier terms

77 *cursitory* cursory 82 *accept* accepted; *peremptory* authoritative 90 *consign* consent 93 *Happily* haply, perchance 94 *nicely* punctiliously 96 *capital* chief

Such as will enter at a lady's ear
And plead his love suit to her gentle heart?

KATHERINE Your majesty shall mock at me. I cannot speak your England.

KING HENRY O fair Katherine, if you will love me soundly with your French heart, I will be glad to hear you confess it brokenly with your English tongue. Do you like me, Kate?

KATHERINE Pardonnez-moi, I cannot tell wat is 'like me.'

KING HENRY An angel is like you, Kate, and you are like an angel.

111 KATHERINE Que dit-il? Que je suis semblable à les anges?

113 ALICE Oui, vraiment, sauf vostre grace, ainsi dit-il.

KING HENRY I said so, dear Katherine, and I must not blush to affirm it.

KATHERINE O bon Dieu! les langues des hommes sont pleine de tromperies.

KING HENRY What says she, fair one? that the tongues of men are full of deceits?

ALICE Oui, dat de tongues of de mans is be full of deceits. Dat is de princesse.

121 KING HENRY The princess is the better Englishwoman. I' faith, Kate, my wooing is fit for thy understanding. I am glad thou canst speak no better English; for if thou couldst, thou wouldst find me such a plain king that thou wouldst think I had sold my farm to buy my crown. I know no ways to mince it in love but directly to say, 'I love you.' Then, if you urge me farther than to say, 'Do
128 you in faith?' I wear out my suit. Give me your answer, i' faith, do: and so clap hands and a bargain. How say you, lady?

111–12 *Que . . . anges?* what does he say? That I am like the angels? **113** *Oui . . . dit-il* yes, truly, save your grace, so he says **121** *better Englishwoman* (because disdainful of flattery) **128** *wear . . . suit* exhaust my terms of courtship

KATHERINE Sauf vostre honneur, me understand well.

KING HENRY Marry, if you would put me to verses or to
dance for your sake, Kate, why, you undid me. For the
one I have neither words nor measure; and for the other
I have no strength in measure, yet a reasonable measure
in strength. If I could win a lady at leapfrog, or by vault-
ing into my saddle with my armor on my back, under the 137
correction of bragging be it spoken, I should quickly leap
into a wife. Or if I might buffet for my love, or bound
my horse for her favors, I could lay on like a butcher and
sit like a jackanapes, never off. But, before God, Kate, I 141
cannot look greenly, not gasp out my eloquence, nor I 142
have no cunning in protestation, only downright oaths
which I never use till urged, nor never break for urging.
If thou canst love a fellow of this temper, Kate, whose
face is not worth sunburning, that never looks in his
glass for love of anything he sees there, let thine eye be
thy cook. I speak to thee plain soldier. If thou canst love 148
me for this, take me; if not, to say to thee that I shall die,
is true; but for thy love, by the Lord, no; yet I love thee
too. And while thou liv'st, dear Kate, take a fellow of
plain and uncoined constancy, for he perforce must do 152
thee right, because he hath not the gift to woo in other
places. For these fellows of infinite tongue that can
rhyme themselves into ladies' favors, they do always
reason themselves out again. What! A speaker is but a
prater; a rhyme is but a ballad. A good leg will fall, a 157
straight back will stoop, a black beard will turn white, a
curled pate will grow bald, a fair face will wither, a full
eye will wax hollow; but a good heart, Kate, is the sun
and the moon; or rather, the sun, and not the moon, for
it shines bright and never changes, but keeps his course
truly. If thou would have such a one, take me; and take
me, take a soldier; take a soldier, take a king. And what

137–38 *under . . . spoken* though to say so may be reproved as bragging 141 *jackanapes* monkey 142 *greenly* wanly 148 *cook* i.e. caterer 152 *uncoined* not prepared for circulation 157 *fall* diminish

say'st thou then to my love? Speak, my fair, and fairly, I pray thee.

KATHERINE Is it possible dat I sould love de ennemie of France?

KING HENRY No, it is not possible you should love the enemy of France, Kate; but in loving me you should love the friend of France, for I love France so well that I will not part with a village of it – I will have it all mine. And, Kate, when France is mine and I am yours, then yours is France and you are mine.

KATHERINE I cannot tell wat is dat.

KING HENRY No, Kate? I will tell thee in French, which I am sure will hang upon my tongue like a new-married wife about her husband's neck, hardly to be shook off. Je quand sur le possession de France, et quand vous avez le possession de moi (let me see, what then? Saint Denis be my speed!), donc vostre est France et vous estes mienne. It is as easy for me, Kate, to conquer the kingdom as to speak so much more French. I shall never move thee in French, unless it be to laugh at me.

KATHERINE Sauf vostre honneur, le François que vous parlez, il est meilleur que l'Anglois lequel je parle.

KING HENRY No, faith, is't not, Kate. But thy speaking of my tongue, and I thine, most truly-falsely, must needs be granted to be much at one. But, Kate, dost thou understand thus much English? Canst thou love me?

KATHERINE I cannot tell.

KING HENRY Can any of your neighbors tell, Kate? I'll ask them. Come, I know thou lovest me; and at night when you come into your closet, you'll question this gentlewoman about me, and I know, Kate, you will to her dispraise those parts in me that you love with your heart; but, good Kate, mock me mercifully, the rather,

178–79 *Je quand . . . moi* (Henry's bad attempt to paraphrase ll. 172–73)
184–85 *Sauf . . . parle* save your honor, the French you speak is better than the English I speak 193 *closet* private room

gentle princess, because I love thee cruelly. If ever thou
beest mine, Kate, as I have a saving faith within me tells
me thou shalt, I get thee with scambling, and thou must 199
therefore needs prove a good soldier-breeder. Shall not thou and I, between Saint Denis and Saint George, compound a boy, half French, half English, that shall go to Constantinople and take the Turk by the beard? Shall we not? What say'st thou, my fair flower-de-luce?

KATHERINE I do not know dat.

KING HENRY No; 'tis hereafter to know, but now to promise. Do but now promise, Kate, you will endeavor
for your French part of such a boy, and for my English
moiety take the word of a king and a bachelor. How 209
answer you, la plus belle Katherine du monde, mon 210
trèscher et devin déesse?

KATHERINE Your majestee ave fausse French enough to deceive de most sage demoiselle dat is en France.

KING HENRY Now, fie upon my false French! By mine honor in true English, I love thee, Kate; by which honor I dare not swear thou lovest me; yet my blood begins to
flatter me that thou dost, notwithstanding the poor and
untempering effect of my visage. Now beshrew my 218
father's ambition! He was thinking of civil wars when he got me; therefore was I created with a stubborn outside, with an aspect of iron, that when I come to woo ladies, I fright them. But in faith, Kate, the elder I wax the better I shall appear. My comfort is that old age, that ill layer-up of beauty, can do no more spoil upon my face. Thou hast me, if thou hast me, at the worst; and thou shalt wear me, if thou wear me, better and better; and therefore tell me, most fair Katherine, will you have me? Put off your maiden blushes; avouch the thoughts of your heart with the looks of an empress; take me by

199 *scambling* scrambling for possessions, snatching 209 *moiety* half 210–11 *la ... déesse* the most beautiful Katherine of the world, my very dear and divine goddess 218 *untempering* unpropitiating

the hand, and say, 'Harry of England, I am thine!' which word thou shalt no sooner bless mine ear withal but I will tell thee aloud, 'England is thine, Ireland is thine, France is thine, and Henry Plantagenet is thine';
234 who, though I speak it before his face, if he be not fellow with the best king, thou shalt find the best king of good fellows. Come, your answer in broken music! for thy voice is music and thy English broken; therefore, queen of all, Katherine, break thy mind to me in broken English. Wilt thou have me?

239 KATHERINE Dat is as it sall please de roi mon père.

KING HENRY Nay, it will please him well, Kate; it shall please him, Kate.

KATHERINE Den it sall also content me.

KING HENRY Upon that I kiss your hand and I call you my queen.

245 KATHERINE Laissez, mon seigneur, laissez, laissez! Ma foi, je ne veux point que vous abaissiez vostre grandeur en baisant le main d'une de vostre seigneurie indigne serviteur. Excusez-moi, je vous supplie, mon très-puissant seigneur.

KING HENRY Then I will kiss your lips, Kate.

KATHERINE Les dames et demoiselles pour estre baisée devant leur nopces, il n'est pas la coutume de France.

KING HENRY Madam my interpreter, what says she?

ALICE Dat it is not be de fashon pour le ladies of France – I cannot tell wat is 'baiser' en Anglish.

KING HENRY To kiss.

256 ALICE Your majestee entendre bettre que moi.

KING HENRY It is not a fashion for the maids in France to kiss before they are married, would she say?

ALICE Oui, vraiment.

234–35 *fellow with* equal to 239 *de . . . père* the king my father 245–49 *Laissez . . . seigneur* desist, my lord, desist, desist! My faith, I do not wish you to lower your dignity by kissing the hand of your lordship's unworthy servant. Excuse me, I pray you, my all-powerful lord 256 *entendre* understands

KING HENRY O Kate, nice customs curtsy to great kings. Dear Kate, you and I cannot be confined within the weak list of a country's fashion. We are the makers of manners, Kate; and the liberty that follows our places stops the mouth of all findfaults, as I will do yours for upholding the nice fashion of your country in denying me a kiss. Therefore patiently, and yielding. *[Kisses her.]* You have witchcraft in your lips, Kate. There is more eloquence in a sugar touch of them than in the tongues of the French Council, and they should sooner persuade Harry of England than a general petition of monarchs. Here comes your father.

Enter the French Power and the English Lords.

BURGUNDY God save your majesty! My royal cousin, teach you our princess English?

KING HENRY I would have her learn, my fair cousin, how perfectly I love her, and that is good English.

BURGUNDY Is she not apt?

KING HENRY Our tongue is rough, coz, and my condition is not smooth; so that, having neither the voice nor the heart of flattery about me, I cannot so conjure up the spirit of love in her that he will appear in his true likeness.

BURGUNDY Pardon the frankness of my mirth if I answer you for that. If you would conjure in her, you must make a circle; if conjure up love in her in his true likeness, he must appear naked and blind. Can you blame her then, being a maid yet rosed over with the virgin crimson of modesty, if she deny the appearance of a naked blind boy in her naked seeing self? It were, my lord, a hard condition for a maid to consign to.

KING HENRY Yet they do wink and yield, as love is blind and enforces.

262 *list* barrier 263 *follows our places* attends our rank 265 *nice* fastidious 277 *condition* personality 284 *blind* (1) sightless, (2) reckless, brutal 288 *consign* consent 289 *wink* shut eyes

BURGUNDY They are then excused, my lord, when they see not what they do.

KING HENRY Then, good my lord, teach your cousin to consent winking.

BURGUNDY I will wink on her to consent, my lord, if you
296 will teach her to know my meaning; for maids well sum-
297 mered and warm kept are like flies at Bartholomew-tide,
blind, though they have their eyes; and then they will
endure handling which before would not abide looking
on.

KING HENRY This moral ties me over to time and a hot summer; and so I shall catch the fly, your cousin, in the latter end, and she must be blind too.

BURGUNDY As love is, my lord, before it loves.

KING HENRY It is so; and you may, some of you, thank love for my blindness, who cannot see many a fair French city for one fair French maid that stands in my way.

307 FRANCE Yes, my lord, you see them perspectively, the
cities turned into a maid; for they are all girdled with
maiden walls that war hath never entered.

KING HENRY Shall Kate be my wife?

FRANCE So please you.

KING HENRY I am content, so the maiden cities you talk
313 of may wait on her. So the maid that stood in the way for
my wish shall show me the way to my will.

FRANCE
We have consented to all terms of reason.

KING HENRY
Is't so, my lords of England?

WESTMORELAND
The king hath granted every article:
His daughter first; and in sequel all,

296 *well summered* i.e. carefully nurtured **297** *like . . . Bartholomew-tide* i.e. sluggish in the heat of summer **307** *perspectively* i.e. through an optic glass (which multiplies images) **313** *wait on her* i.e. come with her as a dowry

According to their firm proposèd natures. 319

EXETER Only he hath not yet subscribèd this: Where
your majesty demands that the King of France, having
any occasion to write for matter of grant, shall name
your highness in this form and with this addition, in
French, 'Nostre très-cher fils Henri, Roi d'Angleterre, 323
Héritier de France'; and thus in Latin, 'Praeclarissimus filius noster Henricus, Rex Angliae et Haeres
Franciae.'

FRANCE
Nor this I have not, brother, so denied
But your request shall make me let it pass.

KING HENRY
I pray you then, in love and dear alliance,
Let that one article rank with the rest,
And thereupon give me your daughter.

FRANCE
Take her, fair son, and from her blood raise up
Issue to me, that the contending kingdoms
Of France and England, whose very shores look pale 334
With envy of each other's happiness,
May cease their hatred, and this dear conjunction
Plant neighborhood and Christian-like accord
In their sweet bosoms, that never war advance
His bleeding sword 'twixt England and fair France.

LORDS Amen!

KING HENRY
Now, welcome, Kate; and bear me witness all
That here I kiss her as my sovereign queen.
Flourish.

QUEEN
God, the best maker of all marriages,
Combine your hearts in one, your realms in one!
As man and wife, being two, are one in love,

319 *firm . . . natures* strict stipulations 323–26 *Nostre . . . France; . . . Praeclarissimus . . . Franciae* our dear son Henry, King of England and heir of France 334 *look pale* i.e. with their chalk cliffs

So be there 'twixt your kingdoms such a spousal
347 That never may ill office, or fell jealousy,
Which troubles oft the bed of blessèd marriage,
349 Thrust in between the paction of these kingdoms
To make divorce of their incorporate league;
That English may as French, French Englishmen,
Receive each other! God speak this Amen!

ALL Amen!

KING HENRY
Prepare we for our marriage; on which day,
My Lord of Burgundy, we'll take your oath,
And all the peers', for surety of our leagues.
Then shall I swear to Kate, and you to me,
And may our oaths well kept and prosp'rous be!

Sennet. Exeunt.

Epi. *Enter Chorus [as Epilogue].*

Thus far, with rough and all-unable pen,
2 Our bending author hath pursued the story,
In little room confining mighty men,
4 Mangling by starts the full course of their glory.
Small time; but in that small most greatly lived
This Star of England. Fortune made his sword,
7 By which the world's best garden he achieved,
And of it left his son imperial lord.
9 Henry the Sixth, in infant bands crowned King
Of France and England, did this king succeed;
Whose state so many had the managing
That they lost France and made his England bleed:
13 Which oft our stage hath shown; and for their sake,
14 In your fair minds let this acceptance take.

347 *ill office* evil dealing 349 *paction* pact
Epi. 2 *bending* bowing, humble 4 *Mangling by starts* misrepresenting in fragments 7 *best garden* i.e. France (cf. V, ii, 36) 9 *infant bands* swaddling clothes 13 *for their sake* i.e. inasmuch as they have pleased you 14 *this* this play

APPENDIX: THE QUARTO AND FOLIO TEXTS

The 1600 quarto of *Henry V*, although twice reprinted, presents a curtailed and corrupt version of the play, probably obtained by memorial reconstruction of the original. It is sometimes maintained that the actors playing the parts of Exeter and Gower were the chief agents in this reconstruction, since the portions of the play where they are on stage are somewhat more accurately preserved than the rest. The quarto is useful in supplying an occasional line or reading in instances where the folio text is clearly defective. The folio text, although reliable in the main, is marred by a number of misprints and a somewhat capricious division into acts. The first act corresponds to acts I and II in modern editions, the second to III, the third to the first six scenes of IV, the fourth to the remainder of IV, and the fifth to V. The modern division is based on the position of the four internal speeches by the Chorus. The logic of this solution may be more apparent than real, since it substitutes for the inordinately long first "act" of the folio the inordinately long fourth "act" of modern editions. It is possible that the choruses were originally no more than a narrative convenience, their number formally insignificant.

In the present edition, there is a minimum of departure from the folio text except for the usual modernization of spelling and punctuation, the normalization of speech-prefixes, and occasional relineation. (In the folio, Pistol's speeches are printed in prose, apparently because his thumping iambics appear in the midst of the prose dialogue of his comic associates.) Such proper names as "Dauphin," "Burgundy," "Calais," "Harfleur," etc. have been consistently substituted for the original "Dolphin," "Burgonie" (or "Burgogne"), "Callice," "Harflew," etc. Fluellen's Welsh dialect has been normalized by the consistent use of "orld" for "world," "Cheshu" for "Jesu," and "p" for initial "b" in stressed syllables. However, Macmorris' "sh" for "s" is allowed to remain intermittent.

Contrary to general practice in modern editions of this play, the passages in French are no more extensively modified than the passages in English. Archaic and familiar grammatical forms, as well as errors in grammar and idiom, have been retained. The advantage of this kind of fidelity to the copy-text is that more of the original quality and flavour of Shakespeare's French is preserved than is possible when modern copybook correctness is substituted, and, in one instance (IV, ii, 2–6), an original meaning is restored. After expending much effort upon my attempt to restore Princess Katherine's English lesson (III, iv) to its Shakespearean form, I found that I had been anticipated in most details by Nikolaus Delius.

The following is a complete list of all substantive departures from the text of the folio of 1623 (F). The adopted readings in italics from the quarto of 1600 (Q) and from the later folios and the editors are followed by the folio readings in roman.

I, ii, 38 *succedant* (F2) succedaul 45, 52 *Elbe* (Capell) Elue 74 *Lingard* (Sisson) Lingare 82 *Ermengard* (Sisson) Ermengare 94 *imbar* (F3) imbarre 131 *blood* (F3) Bloods 163 *her* (Capell) their 209 *many several* (Q) many 213 *End* (Q) And

II, i, 22 *mare* (Q) name 26 *How . . . Pistol* (joined in F to preceding speech by Bardolph; assigned in Q to Nym) 39, 40 *Iceland* (Steevens) Island 68 *Coupe la* (Dyce) Couple a 69 *thee defy* (Q) defie thee 76 *enough.* (Pope) enough to 79 *you,* (Hanmer) *your* 101–02 *I . . . betting* (Q) Omitted 112 *that's* (Q) that 114 *Ah* (Pope) A

II, ii, 75 *hath* (Q) have 87 *furnish him* (F2) furnish 108 *whoop* (Theobald) hoope 114 *All* (Hanmer) And 122 *lion gait* (Capell) Lyon-gate 139 *mark the* (Malone) make thee 147 *Henry* (Q) Thomas 148 *Masham* (Rowe) Marsham 159 *Which I* (F2) which 176 *have sought* (Q) sought

II, iii, 3, 6 *earn* (Camb.) erne 16 *'a babbled* (Theobald) a Table 24 *upward and upward* (Q) vp-peer'd and vpward 44 *word* (Q) world

II, iv, 68 *followed* (Pope) followèd 79 *borrowed* (Pope) borrowèd 107 *privèd* (Walter) privy 109 *swallowed* (Pope) swallowèd 134 *difference* (Camb.) diff'rence

III, Cho., 4 *Hampton* (Theobald) Dover 6 *fanning* (Rowe) fayning 12 *furrowed* (Rowe) furrowèd

III, i, 7 *summon* (Rowe) commune 17 *noble* (Malone) noblish 24 *men* (F4) me 32 *Straining* (Rowe) Straying

III, ii, 15 *hie* (Q) high 18 *preach* (Hanmer, as also for some similar normalizations of Welsh accent following) breach 58, 127 *petter* better 64, 74 *orld* world 65 *peard* beard 100 *trompet* trumpet 106 *ay'll lig* (Camb.) Ile ligge 107 *ay'll* (Camb.) Ile 120 *poth* both 121 *pirth* birth 129 *pold* bold

III, iii, 16 *Arrayed* (Pope) Arrayèd 32 *heady* (F2) headly 35 *Defile* (Rowe) Desire

III, iv, 2 *parles* (Warburton) parlas 4 *enseigner* (F2) ensigniez *j'apprends* (This ed.) ie apprend 6, 17, 24 *est* (F2) & 7 *Et les doigts* (misplaced in a separate speech givęn to *Alice* in F; corrected by Theobald) *Et les* (Capell) E le 8 *Alice* (Theobald) Kat *Les* (Capell) Le *les* (Capell) e 9 *souviendrai* (F2) souemeray 11 *Katherine* (Theobald) Alice (F, with proper assignment to Katherine restored at *j'ai gagné*) *de fingres* (Capell) le Fingres 11, 13 *les* (Capell) le 14 *Les* (F2) Le 20 *Et le* (F2) E de 36 *la* (F2) de 38 *N'avez-vous pas* (F2) N'ave vos y *déjà* (Warburton) desia 40 *Non* (Warburton) Nome 44 *Sauf* (Rowe) Sans 45 *dis-je* (F2) de ie 46 *le* (Capell) les *la* (Capell) de *robe* (Rowe) roba 47, 48 *De . . . de* (Capell) Le . . . le 50 *les* (F2) le 51 *ces* (F2) ce *les* (F2) le 52 *Foh!* (Camb.) fo *de* (Capell) le 53 *Néantmoins* (F2) neant moys 55 *de count* (Warburton) le count

III, v, 7 *scions* (Var., 1803) Syens 11 *de* (F2) du 43 *Vaudemont* (F2) Vandemont 45 *Foix* (Capell) Loys 46 *knights* (Theobald conj.; Pope) Kings

III, vi, 4, 11 *pridge* Bridge 10 *plessed* blessed 10, 15, 82 *orld* world 30, 31 *plind* blind 30 *her* (Q) his 53 *prother* Brother 98 *Pardolph* Bardolph 100 *plows* blows 108 *lenity* (Q) Leuitie

III, vii, 12 *pasterns* (F2) postures *Ça* (Theobald) ch' 57 *lief* (Capell) liue 62 *vomissement* (F2) vemissement 63 *et la truie* (Rowe) est la leuye

IV, Cho., 16 *name* (Tyrwhitt conj.; Steevens) nam'd 20 *cripple* (Theobald) creeple– 27 *Presenteth* (Hanmer) Presented

IV, i, 3 *Good* (F3) God 65 *Cheshu* Jesu 66 *orld* world 71 *pabble* babble 91 *Thomas* (Theobald) John 231 *What is* (Knight) What? is *adoration* (F2) Odoration 239 *Think'st*

(Rowe) Thinks 261 *Hyperion* (F2) Hiperio 277 *if* (Tyrwhitt conj.; Steevens) of 282 *bestowed* (Pope) bestowèd

IV, ii, 4 *eaux* (Theobald) ewes 5 *les* (This ed.) le 6 *Cieux* (Munro, as 'cieu') Cien 11 *dout* (Rowe) doubt 25 *'gainst* (F2) against 49 *gimmaled* (Delius) Iymold

IV, iii, 13–14 *And... valor* (after l. 11 in F; correction by Theobald supported by Q) 48 *And... day* (Q) Omitted 59 *rememberèd* (Rowe) rememb'red 99 *buried* (Eds.) buryèd

IV, iv, 12 *pitié* (F2) pitez 14 *Or* (Hanmer) For 34 *de* (F2) a *faites* (Malone) faite 37 *cuppe le* (This ed.) cuppele 39 *O'er-* (This ed.) Or 51 *néantmoins* (F2) neant-mons 52 *l'avez promis* (Malone) layt a promets 55 *remercîmens* (F2) remercious *j'ai tombé* (This ed.) Je intombe 57 *distingué* (Capell) distinie 65 *Suivez* (Rowe) Saaue

IV, v, 2 *perdu... est perdu* (Rowe) perdia... et perdie 3 *Mort de* (Rowe) Mor Dieu 12 *honor* (Q) Omitted 16 *by a slave* (Q) a base slave 24 *Exeunt* (Eds.) Exit

IV, vi, 15 *And* (Q) He 34 *mistful* (Theobald) mixtful

IV, vii, 24, 28 *poth* both 44 *pelly* belly 73 *the* (Capell) with 96 *padge* badge 106 *Cheshu* Jeshu 110 *God* (F3) Good 119 *'a live* (Capell) aliue 134 *plack* blacke

IV, viii, 10, 41 *orld* world 32 *peggarly* beggarly 58 *pelly* belly 61 *petter* better 94 *Foix* (Capell) Foyes 108 *we* (F2) me

V, i, 5 *peggarly* beggarly 6 *orld* world 9 *pid* bid 10 *preed* breed 11 *pold* bold 20 *beseech* peseech 37 *Pite* Bite 49 *proken* broken 81 *swear* (F3) swore

V, ii, 12 *England* (F2) Ireland 45 *fumitory* (F4) Femetary 50 *all* (Rowe) withall 77 *cursitory* (Wilson) curselarie 185 *est* (Pope) & *meilleur* (Hanmer) melius 246 *abaissiez* (Johnson) abbaise *grandeur* (F2) grandeus 247 *de vostre* (Camb.) nostre *seigneurie* (Camb.) Seigneur 252 *coutume* (Rowe) costume 255 *baiser* (Hanmer) buisse 259 *vraiment* (Hanmer) verayment 309 *never* (Rowe) Omitted 324 *Héritier* (Rowe) Heretere 349 *paction* (Theobald) Pation